ARDATH MAYHAR

CLOSELY KNIT IN SCARLATT

Complete and Unabridged

LINFORD
Leicester

First published in Great Britain

First Linford Edition
published 2012

British Library CIP Data

Mayhar, Ardath.
  Closely knit in Scarlatt. - -
  (Linford mystery library)
  1. Suspense fiction.
  2. Large type books.
  I. Title II. Series
  813.5'4–dc23

  ISBN 978–1–4448–1114–8

Published by
F. A. Thorpe (Publishing)
Anstey, Leicestershire

Set by Words & Graphics Ltd.
Anstey, Leicestershire
Printed and bound in Great Britain by
T. J. International Ltd., Padstow, Cornwall

This book is printed on acid-free paper

Dedicated to all the wicked old ladies
like me, who know how to handle
any situation that comes along;
and to all the dear innocents who
help us across the street — and pick
up our knitting . . .

Prologue

The long black Lincoln slid to a stop, wipers moving rapidly, dissipating the greasy mist of rain. The man who hurried from the portico of the mansion beyond the iron fence carried a huge umbrella, which he held solicitously over the gnome-sized bundle of overcoats that emerged from the car.

Before they reached the shelter of the portico, quiet men in dark overcoats appeared from the interior of the limousine and posted themselves at strategic points about the garden. They could do nothing about the forest that stood, dark with rain, on every side, yet they watched the fringes of the trees as intently as they did the curving expanse of the patterned brick drive.

The rain intensified, as other quietly expensive automobiles arrived, deposited their riders, and withdrew to the other side of the garden wall to the shelter of an immense garage. There the drivers huddled about an electric heater, gossiping, shooting craps, alert to any signal that they might be needed.

Inside the mansion, people who seldom came face to face were meeting for the first time in years. Cavalieri from Las Vegas, Tomassini from Boston, O'Herlihy from Houston (and Corpus Christi) sat with their peers. They were all big men in their fields of influence, yet many of them were now shrunken with age, looking like a set of distinguished mummies, propped up for some esoteric theatrical production.

Twenty old men sat around the antique refectory table in a room that dwarfed the massive Italian furniture. A fire roared and spat in a fireplace that would have been at home in a medieval castle.

The gentle whisper of central heating added its warmth to comfort the aged bones of those who had come to this conference. Even with so much heat, several huddled thick sweaters about their shoulders as they waited for the meeting to begin.

A manservant removed coffee cups and wineglasses as the murmur of conversation died away. An air of alertness swept over the ancient group as the massive man who sat at the head of the table leaned forward and picked up a file of papers.

'It will be necessary to apply pressure to key people in the Ministry in London,' he began. 'Great Britain is not yet securely organized by our people there. In order to achieve our goals we must gain some leverage. Someone who is extremely knowledgeable in the area of military intelligence, yet who is not guarded constantly, would make an excellent hostage.

'We have learned that Benjamin Scarlatt has retired to private life, though he still consults with the Ministry when there is need for his expertise. By midsummer he will be taking a cruise for his health. His doctor has been less than discreet in the company of his servants, and we know he will insist upon this.

'By abducting him, we may become able to set our operations into motion, using the leverage that will give us over the various law enforcement agencies in Great Britain.'

Tomassini stirred, his dark eyes bright amid the wrinkles of his gnomish face. 'Why Scarlatt? I've heard of him, of course. He was in Parliament after he left the Ministry, but he has retired even from that position. Why do you think he will be so useful?'

Gianello looked down at the papers he held and smiled. 'Scarlatt has never retired from his true profession, which is covert work for M.I.5. True, he went into law after the War, and then into politics, but he has always been important to British security.

'He is privy to information that the British government cannot risk having come to light. Now that he has, we believe, truly retired from everything, he should not be guarded closely, but what he contains within his mind will be with him until he dies. Much of that has to be explosive in nature, given the present global situation.'

'So we don't just put out a contract . . .'

mused Cavalieri.

'That would gain us nothing. It is by learning what he knows and using it to blackmail key government officials that we will begin gaining ground in England. Scarlatt dead is a great loss to his country, but those secrets would die with him. Scarlatt alive and in unknown hands will frighten governments, and is a tool that anyone in Business would drool over.'

'Surely he will be guarded in some way,' rumbled O'Herlihy. 'Even the British wouldn't risk him, would they? And there's no easy escape from a ship at sea, with so many navies here and there. How do you propose to get at him?'

Gianello smiled again. His rich voice was creamy as he purred, 'Have you ever heard of the Knit Lady?'

Cavalieri jumped. Two of the others around the big table looked thoughtful but said nothing.

Gianello spread the file's contents before him on the polished mahogany. 'There is one assassin who is known, literally, to nobody, even those who hire him. He obviously calls himself the Knit Lady in order to mislead everyone, and he achieves results that even the big-time pros cannot equal.

'There has never been even a hint of a description of the man. No clue ever led anywhere except into a stone wall. There have been at least five Knit Lady hits that cost other professionals their lives or their freedom, and at least two KGB agents are no longer working because of him. Never once has there been a slip.'

'How long has he been in the game?' asked O'Herlihy, whose gnarled fingers were tapping impatiently on the table. 'How do you know so much about him-her, whatever, anyway?'

'He has been in the profession for some time. I know those who first employed him. I am an associate of the Group who recruited and trained him. They are close-mouthed about their assassin, but it is clear they use him only in extremely important and dangerous situations. He was recommended to me by . . . ' — he peered about at his fellows — ' . . . Al Genno.'

6

Several of the men caught their breaths sharply. Cavalieri nodded slowly. 'So. The Group has used her? Him? I don't like using someone we have no way to control.'

'Genno was very close with information, but he absolutely guaranteed satisfaction. The Knit Lady usually does hits only, but he can do just about anything, Genno says. We want him to get close to Scarlatt, get chummy with him. To be in position to slip him a needle, when the time comes.'

'So we send this Knit Lady person on the cruise Scarlatt is taking.' O'Herlihy's fingers were now still, and his expression was interested. 'Shouldn't be any problem.'

'This is not a cruise you sign up for and pay your fare. This has been organized by prominent doctors in this country and abroad. Many of their wealthy patients who are either too old or too disabled to take a regular trip want to travel. A Liberian cruise ship has been chartered, the doctors are in charge of arrangements, and several are going along to attend the patients, right there on the ship. Genno tells me the Knit Lady can qualify, though on what grounds he did not say. Nobody else I know could possibly do that.'

Tomassini interrupted. 'I've got a lock on a big society doctor. Old family, big patient load of wealthy people. Uses coke. I supply him free, and he does me favors when I need anything in his line of work. Should be able to work this through him, don't you think? He never asks questions.'

Heads nodded, except for one. D'Indio, at the foot of the table, was the only holdout. 'I want to know more. I want to hear about something this guy really did, something we all knew about and that we didn't suspect wasn't on the up and up.'

Gianello nodded. 'I will give you one. I cannot prove it, nor could Genno, but it is what the Knit Lady was hired to do. It got done, and there is word on the pipeline that the terrorists involved never intended to do the thing that resulted.'

He fumbled through the pages. 'Does anyone here recall Balfour G'dami?'

Brows wrinkled with thought. Then Cavalieri said, 'That bum from Africa! Dictator who came over here to beg for arms to put down a revolution, I think.

Got blown to hell down in Texas some-place, when he was visiting his old teacher from missionary days. That the guy?'

Gianello grunted. 'That's the one. He was targeted by a bunch of his own people — rebels who refugeed here and waited for a chance to get at him. Those terrorists who took the fall were wanting him for a hostage to get some of their own people released, back in Upper Balvi.

'However, he was killed with a weapon that could be traced to them, and they were on the spot, both dead and alive. It was easier to let them take the rap than to untangle the mess. That was a Knit Lady job. The guys who put out the contract, Genno tells me, paid off like a shot and never asked a question.'

'Those people had a lot of hostages, if I remember right,' Cavalieri said. 'Nobody among them had any idea who killed the guards and released them, did they?'

'They were all kinds, country people, tourists, kids, blacks and whites, and they were stopped on a country highway at twilight. Masked men and women with Uzis. The hostages were so scared and confused they couldn't tell anything worth knowing.

'A few insisted there had been eleven of them at first, but when it all got sorted out, there were only ten. The police thought they miscounted, but I think the eleventh must have been the Knit Lady.'

A hum of talk went around the table. Small arguments flared and died down again. Gianello sat silent in his big chair. His smug expression told anyone interested that he was confident that his plan would be adopted, no matter how these lesser kingpins sputtered and fumed.

He was correct. By the time a silent-footed butler came into the room to replenish the logs in the fireplace, the arguments had ended. The thing was put to a vote, and unanimously the men who controlled the Brokers decided to assign the Knit Lady to arrange the abduction of Benjamin Scarlatt, KCB.

★   ★   ★

Food was served afterward, and the old men drank a bit more port than was good for them. Then they were put back into their posh vehicles by the silent young men who brought them, and driven back to their own power-bases.

Among those clearing away the debris of the meeting were two who served more than one master. They had worked for Gianello for years and knew everything about his business and his house. They saved every scrap of paper found after one of the infrequent meetings of the Brokers.

In time, the fruits of their scavenging found a way into hands the old men would never have believed existed.

★   ★   ★

There were things the old men of the Brokers could not know about their proposed employee. The Knit Lady was certainly not a man. She was not young. And she had her own complicated but stringent code of ethics.

She also didn't take blind orders worth a tinker's damn.

1

If anyone had told Olive Shaughnessy that she would grow up to be an assassin, she would have laughed him to scorn. The young Olive was a light-footed, light-hearted girl who was ready for whatever life had in store for her.

She was too bright for her own good, as her teachers at the school at St. Ursula's Convent told her more than once. Her parents swore she was determined to the point of being pig-headed.

Still, she was ready to learn anything, if they could convince her it was important or interesting. She was kind, in a teasing sort of way, and she had an uproarious sense of humour.

It might have been that, more than anything, that drew Francesco Rienzi to court her. There were prettier girls (though he insisted there weren't many of those). There were girls who were easier to persuade to pet or to go into the back seats of automobiles. Olive refused to make such expeditions with anyone. She wasn't bright for nothing, and stubbornness helped too.

Now, sitting in her kitchen, listening to the stertorious breathing of her husband, she thought it was the fact that she made him laugh that had attracted him. For her own part, it had been his dark and tragic air that snared her fancy.

She poured herself another cup of coffee and sighed. Francis had good reason to be unhappy. After lending his scapegrace uncle all his savings, the young Francesco had found himself left behind in Italy to tend his grandparents alone.

Not a dime ever came back to him from the golden shores of America. Even now, fifty years later, Ottavio Rienzi had yet to repay any of the sum his nephew had given him in order to save his life and allow him to flee his native country.

As soon as her duty to Francis was done, Olive intended to kill Ottavio Rienzi. Her soul might well end up in Hell, as her long-ago teachers had threatened, but if so that was quite all right. A man who could allow his near kin to suffer and die without coming to see him even once, a man who could let that nephew lack for proper medical attention when he knew he owed him the money that might prolong his life — that man deserved death.

A quiet moan from the bedroom beyond the kitchen caught her attention. Olive's fingers gripped the cup until they turned pale and bloodless. If only Francis had let her put him into the hospital! Somehow she would have managed to pay his expenses, she knew, but he feared debt more than death, and there was no free medical care for one who had never gained his U.S. citizenship.

She rose, rinsed out the cup, and set it in the cabinet. Then she moved to the door. Francis was quiet again by the time she entered the room and sat quietly in her low chair to watch him struggle for breath.

The thought of Rienzi sitting in his posh office at the U.N., respected now, and influential in the position Francesco's money had made possible, made her want to spit.

So what if she had to sell the house and the furniture and everything else? She'd go out and scrub floors, for homemaking skills were all she had to show, if it would ease Francis's suffering. But he refused hospitalization, and he only allowed the doctor, who was a neighbour, to come when they had the cash to pay for his calls.

This was cankering inside her while she waited for her husband to die.

His eyes opened and focused on her. Francis looked apologetic, and she knew he was thinking about what would happen to her when he was gone. In her sixties, with the debts she had made secretly to keep him in pain-killers, she knew it wasn't going to be easy.

'Cara?' His voice was even weaker than before.

'Yes, Francesco. I'm here. Do you need anything?'

'No.' He breathed very hard for a moment. 'You had . . . your . . . coffee?'

'Yes. I'll be here for a while now. You try to sleep.'

He closed his eyes, and his chest moved with the effort of breathing, while her knitting needles clicked softly and a scarlet scarf grew longer and longer between her fingers. Then she paused, listening hard.

His breathing actually seemed to be easing. Could it be that he had passed some crisis, that he might be improving? Her heart thudded but she calmed it. This was no time for hope, and she knew it too well.

Francesco's breathing stopped, just like that. No death-rattle, no struggle, simply silence where there had been sound.

She rose, dropped the knitting, and knelt beside the bed. His hand, too pale and thin to be that familiar one she had known so long, hung down beside the coverlet. She took it in both hers and laid her cheek against it.

Now he was with their four stillborn babies. She would not cry — together, surely they would be happy. There would be time for crying when Francis's death was avenged. In their years together, she had learned the concept of vendetta.

She stood, her arthritic knee stiff and sore, and laid her husband's hands across his chest, one covering the other. She drew the sheet over his face and turned to go next door after the doctor, who had come home while she sat in the kitchen.

She knew she would have to walk all over town while settling their affairs, selling the house, paying the last of the bills. She was used to it; their Ford had gone two years before to pay for treatment that did no good at all.

Her coal of internal anger kept her going. Only a few old friends attended Francesco's funeral, which was as quick and as inexpensive as she could manage and stay with the law of the Church. Some looked odd when the service was over so quickly, but she disregarded that.

The flame of rage burned inside her, and she nurtured it while attending to the things she must do.

'I will go to the city,' she told those who inquired. 'Francis has relatives there.'

It was not a lie. Ottavio Rienzi and his family lived there.

2

Standing for the last time on the doorstep of her empty house, Olive felt cold and weary. It was frightening to be old and alone and faced with such a difficult and terrible duty. But she had no home now. That had been sold, and she knew Francis rested more easily if he knew all their debts were now paid.

She hefted her single suitcase, hung her knitting bag over her arm, and trudged up the street toward the bus station. She had the money for a ticket to New York. There was enough, she hoped, for a cheap room and food for perhaps a month or so. Surely she would be able to find some kind of work in that length of time.

Olive went first to the U.N. building, but there was no vacancy on the cleaning staff. At last she got a job scrubbing floors in another office building. That allowed her to find a tiny room with a hotplate, and there she rested from her labours and bided her time.

To her surprise, the hard work seemed to improve her health. Though her knees ached abominably, she found she was able to walk farther and to do more when she got to work than had been true in several years.

Encouraged, she pushed herself as much as possible, and got herself into very good shape for a woman of her age. It wasn't going to be easy to kill Rienzi, she knew, even though he was considerably older than she. He had been his parents' youngest child, and Francesco had been the son of a much older brother. A scant three years separated their ages, but Olive had been ten years younger than her husband.

She wasn't tall. She was stocky and tough, but that might not be enough. She needed to be strong as well.

When the arthritis hurt badly, she ignored it. Rage was a good painkiller, she found.

★ ★ ★

She applied regularly at the U.N., and in eight months time a position came open on the cleaning staff. She got it, simply because of her persistence. They set her to cleaning offices, and in time she was rotated to the floor where Ottavio Rienzi's office was located. That night she went home and poured herself a glass of cheap white wine. A celebration was in order, though there was no one with whom she might share it. She went to bed a bit tipsy, but more at peace than she had felt in almost a year.

Night after night her work was the same. She toddled into the building with her bag, which contained a coverall and her knitting bag. She scrubbed and dusted, emptied waste paper baskets, straightened furniture, moving from office to office. When she took her break, she always retired to the employees' lounge, where she knitted for fifteen minutes exactly. The security people on that floor said they could set their watches by her.

Jonah, who was on at night on the floor she cleaned, grew so accustomed to her that she felt he didn't notice her at all, after the first week. When she greeted him, coming on duty, he only nodded, seldom looking up from his paperback mystery novel. That suited her plans perfectly.

Night after night she tapped at Rienzi's door, got no answer, and cleaned his office scrupulously. She had heard that he worked late when there was a session that pertained to his country's interests, and she intended to wait for one of those late nights. That would happen, sooner or later.

Three months went by with agonizing slowness. Olive found that blaze of hatred flickering, cooling. How long could she hold onto that intense rage? Lying in bed at night, she deliberately thought of Francis's pain-wracked illness and those last days of worry when he knew she must be left destitute. She relived those days in the chair beside his bed, listening to his struggle to breathe. She found that stoked her fires as nothing else could do.

★   ★   ★

Late that fall, she tapped at Rienzi's door, expecting no reply. 'Go away!' said a voice. 'This office is in use. It cannot be cleaned tonight.'

She smiled at the door, feeling a surge of warmth rise in her body. Smoothing her face, she turned toward Jonah's post and shrugged. 'I'll go down the other hall until he's done,' she said.

'Unh-hunh!' Jonah didn't look up from his book.

Olive trundled her cart of supplies around the corner and partway down the hall. Then she crept back to the second door leading into the office of Rienzi's secretary, which was around the corner from the one leading directly into his office.

Her passkey slid silently into the lock, which she oiled every time she cleaned. The door opened without a sound, and she closed it behind her in an instant. Checking that her knitting bag was secure at her belt, she slipped across the twilit room toward the inner door. A line of light marked its edges.

She touched the handle with a hand

protected by a cleaning cloth. It too was locked, but one of her keys fitted it, for she had tried all the locks while she waited for her chance. The lock turned with a faint click, and she went through the door and closed it behind her.

Rienzi looked up, annoyed. For an instant his likeness to his nephew stopped her cold. Then he spoke, his face red with anger.

'Go clean another office!' he snapped. He spoke as if to an animal, and that removed any resemblance to her gentle Francesco.

Olive stood looking at him across the wide expanse of mahogany. 'You don't recognize me? But that is not surprising. You didn't come to Francesco's funeral — or even send flowers. Why should you recognize his wife?' she asked.

He stiffened, his face growing darker and more congested. 'You have no claim upon me! Go away, or I shall call Security!'

She snorted. 'Such a loving family man,' she purred. 'You did so much for — or was it to? — your nephew, letting him die penniless, when you owed him money. The family would have been proud of you, Ottavio.' She moved around the corner of the desk toward him.

'If your grandparents were alive, they would curse you. They are gone, but I am here, and I shall do that for them.'

Rienzi rolled his chair backwards, away from her, until it bumped against the floor-to-ceiling bookcase behind him. He leaned his head against the padded leather of the high-backed chair and reached for the telephone.

But Olive had the long steel knitting needle already in her hand. Even as Rienzi's fingers touched the phone, she moved. The bright steel was quenched in his throat, pinning him to the chair-back, voiceless.

His mouth worked, but no sound came out. Rienzi's eyes were glazed with terror, seeing his approaching death, as he stared up at her.

His hands flapped, seeking some weapon, some help . . . and then they went limp.

She balled her red yarn about the

wound, catching most of the blood. Then she wiped her needle and put the wad of scarlet into a plastic bag inside the knitting bag. She put on her rubber gloves, which she had brought in her coverall pocket, and took up a paper knife from the desk, ramming that into the needle-wound in Rienzi's throat.

She checked to make certain she had left no sign of her presence in the office. Then she returned to the hall through the outer office and took up her work again, after washing her hands in the scrub bucket.

She cleaned all the offices quickly and thoroughly. When the time for her break came, she went to the lounge and washed out her knitting, scrubbed her needle, and checked every item of her clothing for bloodstains. She found no trace. She filled the scrub bucket with clean water and sat down to knit for her allotted time.

She did not return to Rienzi's door that night. When she said goodnight to Jonah, she pretended to remember that omission. 'My lord! I forgot to go back and clean that Eyetalian fellow's office, and here it is time to go. You think I'll get into trouble?' she asked.

Jonah looked up at last, bored and grumpy. 'He ain't even left yet. I'll check with him before I go, but if he wants his office cleaned, he just better get out in time for you to do it. G'd night.'

When Jonah looked down at his book, everyone knew it was time to leave him be. Olive nodded, smiled, and left.

3

For the first time in over a year, Olive slept dreamlessly, and she didn't wake until early afternoon. When her eyes opened, she lay still for a moment, trying to track down the source of that feeling of well-being. Then she remembered — Rienzi was dead. Francesco could rest easy now.

She washed, dressed, and then, having put it off as long as possible, she turned on the tiny radio she had bought at a pawnshop. It was weak and old and picked up only the strongest stations, and on those she found nothing of interest. She fixed her supper/breakfast and ate with appetite for the first time since her husband's death.

When the time came to set off for work, she gathered her belongings and found her stomach filled with butterflies. Surely by now someone had found Ottavio. Would anyone suspect her? But she must follow through as if she knew nothing.

* * *

The building was as usual in the evening, almost empty except for those still in their own offices. Jonah was reading, as usual, at his post when she came down the corridor with her cleaning things.

It might have been any evening at all. Had she only dreamed that encounter with Rienzi?

She rolled her cart past Jonah, who looked up as she approached.

'I better start with that Eyetalian's office tonight, being as I didn't get to do it last night,' she said. 'How late did he stay, anyway?'

Jonah, for once, was animated, his dull grey eyes alight with excitement, but he played it close for a minute. 'Never left,' he told her, his gaze fixed on her face.

'You mean that idiot's set up house-keeping in that office? I'll never get it clean!'

'No.' Now Jonah's voice was filled with

29

satisfaction. 'He died there last night. If you'd gone in, you'd have found him lyin' in his own blood. Murdered. Or you might've caught the killer and been scragged yourself.' His words held great gusto, and she knew he was relishing having one of his beloved murder mysteries come to life before his eyes.

She let her eyes widen and sagged against the cart as if her knees had gone weak. 'You don't mean it! If I'd gone in there . . . but he was still alive when I knocked on his door. Told me to leave it be. That's why I left it for last and then forgot. My lord! If I'd gone in when I got no answer and . . . it doesn't bear thinking about!'

She didn't have to ask questions. Jonah was primed for an audience, and she stood there and listened.

'Somebody stabbed him through the neck with his own paper knife. It was like a stiletto, you see, just right for the job. There wasn't much blood, they say, and maybe the killer didn't get much on him either. You never in your life saw so much action as there was last night, when I checked on him and got the super to unlock the door and we found the body.'

'It must have been terrible,' she breathed. 'How can you be so calm, after seeing something like that?'

Jonah smirked. Never had he commanded the attention he'd known in the past few hours. Even the praise of a cleaning woman was welcome, if nothing better was at hand, so he regaled Olive with his speculations until she looked at her watch and jumped.

'My lord! I'll be fired for certain if I stay here listening to you. Better get to work. Do they want me to clean up in there?'

He shook his head. 'Sealed it up, they did. Told me to keep everybody out until they give me leave to open it again. Scene of the crime, you know.'

She tried to look suitably impressed. 'Well then, I'll be off. If you hear anything interesting, do let me know. I don't get much news, working nights this way.' She toddled away, pushing her cart.

Olive kept right on working as if nothing had happened. Nobody questioned her or seemed to think she might know anything useful. Old women who cleaned offices, she realized, were invisible. Non-existent. It was something to remember, if she ever decided to do anything else that was illegal.

For six weeks she continued at her job, intending to quit and plead her arthritis as a reason, as soon as her gut instinct told her it was the right time. Before that happened, she found a note stuck onto her locker door.

That sent her heart thumping into her stomach for a second, when she saw the white rectangle taped to the grey-green metal. Nobody had ever written her anything before.

She pottered about until the rest of the women on the crew were gone. Then she opened the stiff envelope and read the single line of type:

CALL THIS NUMBER AT YOUR
EARLIEST CONVENIENCE: 758-309-9796.

She felt weak and chilly; did someone suspect something? But she had nothing that would tempt a blackmailer. This had to be something else. She decided to make the call.

When she finally had the time to reach a public phone, the voice at the other end of the line was gruff, yet somehow anonymous. 'Yes?'

'This is . . . the cleaning woman. I found a note.'

'Ah. Yes. We know.'

'Know what?' she asked, trying to bluff it out.

'What you did to Rienzi.'

There was a long silence, while Olive thought frantically and came up with nothing useful.

The voice said, 'We have watched him for months. We also intended to kill him. You did it first, and very well. Very intelligently. You saved us much trouble, and we are not ungrateful.'

'Why did you want to kill him?' she asked, finding her curiosity overriding her fear.

'He has betrayed more than one, in his time.'

'Oh.' She thought a moment. 'Grateful, you say? In what way?'

'You will receive a token of our gratitude. Also, we may talk again. You are good at what you did. We may find . . . uses . . . for you.'

'Uses?'

'You can go where others cannot. You will never be noticed. You look quite harmless and unsuspicious — oh, yes, there are many uses for such a person. We notice that you can be ruthless, and you are obviously intelligent. We will talk again.' The receiver clicked in her ear.

Two days later a packet came for her in her seldom-used mailbox at the rooming house. It contained ten thousand dollars in small denomination, well-used bills. It was enough to pay off the debts she had incurred since Francis died. Inside the packet was another note, with another telephone number.

A different voice answered, less formal, more American and to-the-point. 'We call you the Knit Lady. You need no names for us. We have another job for you, one of the sort you do so well. It will require training, which we are prepared to provide. It will be well paid. Are you interested?'

She didn't take the time to think it over. Her bills were paid. She had already put her immortal soul in jeopardy by committing a murder she would never dare to confess to any priest. She had no intention of scrubbing floors for the rest of her life.

'I am interested,' she said. 'Just tell me what to do.'

4

Olive's first assignment, they told her, was relatively simple and undemanding. The training needed required only some expert coaching in anatomy. Later, they warned, she would find herself learning difficult and dangerous skills, but for now that would suffice.

The place for her debut was a tiny town with a shirt-tail airport, into which a famous 'hanging judge' would soon fly. In such a small place, it should be easy for her to get near enough to her quarry to accomplish the deed. It required only wit and nerve, and she had brought those with her to her new profession.

She refused to go in blindly. 'I do not kill people who don't need killing,' she warned her new employers. 'I mean it. Don't ever assign me to take out anyone who simply gets in your way. Ottavio Rienzi deserved to die. Does this man?'

Her anatomy instructor looked thoughtful. 'You will receive a call,' he said. 'It will be explained. This, you must know, is unexpected, for not often do we employ assassins with scruples. However, we believe you to be potentially valuable to us, even with your strict provisos; all will be made clear.'

With part of her ten thousand dollars she had rented a better room, and now she had a telephone. It rang, that night, at eight o'clock. 'Go to the branch library near you,' a voice said. 'Look up the records of the Crime Commission for 1983 forward to the present. Find the reports on Justice Longworth. In Volume XVIII you will find an insert of typed material that will give you further references. We do not expect you to take our word for the man's culpability. If this does not satisfy you, forget we asked you to perform this task and wait for further contact.'

The records mentioned showed a pattern she recognized. Life-Sentence Longworth had sentenced many men to death for doing things far less criminal than those he did himself. His hand was out. If it was filled, he went easy on the prisoner. If not, he lived up to his nickname. Only his unmentioned but inevitable holds on those in power kept him on the bench.

She accepted the commission.

★ ★ ★

Olive had never flown before, and she found it an interesting experience. When she transferred to the small local air service in Kansas City, she regretted leaving the powerful ship that had brought her from New York, but the small plane was fast and she soon found herself debarking. The small Missouri town, from the air, looked like a straggle of spilled toys. The airport was tiny.

She had been provided with a solid story, if anyone should ask. Her 'niece' was ill. The woman she found waiting for her was truly sick and needed quite a lot of care. Olive slipped back into that mode easily.

From time to time she walked to town

to pay bills or to buy food and medicine for her ailing relative. That let her get acquainted with the local business people. She decided very early that the courthouse and its environs offered little scope for her work, for it stood in the town square, surrounded by un-busy shops whose proprietors watched everything that happened outside. Not a vehicle or a person passed without identification and comment.

Longworth arrived on time and with some fanfare. He was the guest of honour at a local festivity, and he, too, had relatives in the area. He also visited the courthouse several times and had his picture taken with the District Judge, the County Judge, and any commissioners who managed to corner him.

He stayed for five days, which allowed Olive's 'niece' time to recover enough to spare the services of her 'aunt.' Olive arranged to catch the local air service to Kansas City, which Longworth was also scheduled to take on his departure.

The taxi deposited her at the terminal early, but she checked her single bag, watching the girl as if expecting her to abscond with it. When it disappeared into that Black Hole where bags often go and from which they sometimes return, she gathered up her shiny black purse and her knitting bag and fussed away to one of the couches along the wall.

Once settled into a corner, she took out a formidable mass of scarlet knitting, which trailed a woolly umbilicus back into the bowels of her bag. The click of her needles seemed to soothe her into that hypnotic state that sometimes overtakes old ladies when their hands are occupied and their minds are empty.

The clock on the wall hiccupped slightly at every surge of the hands at the passing of a minute. She seemed not to notice it, and only when the judge's party arrived did she rouse. At that point she tucked her scarlet octopus back into the bag and got ready to move.

Longworth had been drinking, she saw. Good. His florid colouring was brighter than before, and the tip of his nose was rosy. He would go to the restroom before taking off; she could depend on it. Her smile grew fractionally less vague.

Fifteen minutes before the plane was scheduled to arrive, she put her purse into her knitting bag, hung the bag on her arm, and tottered down the dark hall leading to the rest rooms. The Ladies' was empty, which was convenient.

Olive perched on a stool before the wide mirror and waited. After a bit, she pulled from the knitting bag an immaculate linen handkerchief, man-sized, with the initials C.M. embroidered in one corner.

Those were not, of course, her own initials.

Footsteps in the hall brought her to attention. She fumbled in her purse, as if searching for something, but no one entered the ladies' room. The steps passed the door and turned into the men's room next door. She had listened intently, and no one else had entered it since she had been waiting.

Olive checked herself in the mirror, donning her bewildered-little-old-lady expression. Vague gaze, sweet, absent smile, just right. Her grey wig was fluffy with curls, and her clothing was so unobtrusive as to be almost invisible.

She moved out into the corridor, closing the door silently behind her. Then she went to the next door, an expression of shocked apology already on her face, in case her intended prey had fooled her. But a steel knitting needle waited in her hand, ready for action.

The top of Longworth's fashionably long white hair gleamed above the divider separating the urinals from the other facilities. This troubled Olive almost more than killing someone — she had never in her life been inside a men's room.

As Longworth began to turn, she rounded the corner, thrusting the needle into his torso from behind, puncturing his heart with one sure motion. The handkerchief caught any blood that might have spurted, though the wound was so small and the needle so sharp that little flowed. She cleaned the needle on the cloth as she withdrew it, dropping the handkerchief into the waste bin and pulling down paper towels to cover it.

In less than two minutes, she was back

in the corridor, the needle in place in the scarlet scarf. She toddled back into the waiting room, found her corner of the couch occupied, and glared at the man who sat there until he squirmed and finally rose. She darted into place, took out her knitting, and began working at a terrific rate.

Nobody noticed, of course. People do not pay heed to elderly ladies who knit.

The clock hiccupped onward. After a short time, someone in the farewell party said, 'The Judge is taking quite a while. You suppose he's sick?'

The young woman addressed looked concerned. 'He seemed so well, but at his age you really can't tell. Somebody had better check on him.'

The local D.A., a great-nephew, Olive had learned, of the visiting dignitary, volunteered to go back and see. He was back almost at once.

In the resulting confusion, Olive packed up her knitting and her purse and wandered vaguely toward the apron where the small plane would board passengers. The pilot was checking items on a clipboard as he stood beside the craft. He was helpful, as she knew he would be, checking her ticket to make certain that she did intend to go to Kansas City. He helped her up the steep steps into the eight seater, where only one other traveler was sitting, before turning his attention to any other passengers.

★ ★ ★

Olive waited for a long time, for the other scheduled passenger did not show up. After some time the pilot emerged from the terminal, looking harried, and took his place in the cockpit. She smiled when he revved the engines and taxied toward the main runway. She didn't even sigh with relief as they took off.

For the first time in her life, Olive felt she was in charge of her destiny. She had done the job, done it unobtrusively, and her employers would be pleased.

I'm good at my work, she thought, watching the houses and trees dwindle beneath the plane. The clouds closed in

44

below and she leaned back. I've found my profession, a bit late maybe, but there are so many people who really do need to be killed. Smiling, she dozed off, her knitting bag clasped firmly in her lap.

5

Joachim Dawes grunted as he reached the top of the circular steps leading to the neat townhouse. That bad leg got no better, and he knew by now that it never would. He could tell when the weather was going to change, usually two or three days in advance, and he'd learned to trust his bones more than the weather man.

That last assignment had been one for the books, and one from which he probably never would recover fully, even though he was only in early middle age. So he hadn't really kicked when the Agency set him behind a desk. When your life depends on your speed and agility, more often than not, being stuck with a dud leg was a death sentence.

Besides, he was rather enjoying staying in the same city, being able to have a permanent residence, and collect books and records from their storage in the homes of his sisters. He had almost forgotten how enjoyable a home could be.

As he pushed the bell, he wondered exactly why he had been called in. It was unusual for someone on the inactive list. Scalpel opened the door on the fourth ring and managed a civil nod.

He didn't attempt a smile, for Scalpel had been the cause of the almost fatal injury Dawes had suffered. The assignment was botched because of the agent's inattention, and Dawes had never forgiven him. Becoming a cripple in completing a successful task was one thing, but as it turned out, it had all been for nothing.

'Ah, Dawes,' Scalpel said.

That shocked Kim Dawes. He was so used to his code name, Drillbit, being used here at headquarters that his own name put him off balance.

'Good morning, Skelley,' he returned. 'Any notion why the Old Man needs me?'

Scalpel didn't answer. He understood the implied insult when Dawes used his name. Instead of replying, he led Dawes down the elegant hall to the door at the rear. Not to the study, as was usual, but to another white panelled door leading to either a library, Dawes thought, or a small sitting room.

The door opened, instead, into a conservatory filled with exotic blossoms. Orchids, mostly — Shades of Nero Wolfe, he thought. I didn't know the old man was into this sort of thing!

Drillbit managed to greet his superior without showing surprise, which would have amused Axe altogether too much. Nothing ever surprised that one, Dawes was certain, and he didn't intend to betray his own control.

'Sir,' he said. 'Glad to see you.' Then he waited for Axe's reply.

The Old Man was sitting, as usual, in an untidy heap in an overstuffed armchair. For such a light-boned person, he managed to sprawl as if he were as massive as any fictional detective. He looked up and nodded.

'Drillbit. Glad you could come. I have a . . . proposition . . . for you.'

He gestured toward a tapestry-covered chair. Dawes sank into it and relaxed. That was a mistake, and he knew it even as he succumbed to the comfort of the thing, which had been designed for just that effect.

'An assignment?' he asked, his voice noncommittal. That was part of the game.

'Well . . . an assignment of a sort. Not an active, dangerous one, Drillbit. You've had your fill of that, I'm sure, and you've performed handsomely, I must say. No, a bit of courier work, more than anything. Ticklish courier work that can't be given to any of our usual people. Either they are too well known or they are too young and inexperienced for this. May be unexpected variables that need instant assessment and decision-making.'

Axe dug out his ancient stinkard of a pipe from a crumpled pouch and lit it lengthily.

'I was pretty well known as an agent,' Dawes said. 'I was in the field for almost twenty years, after all.'

'But for the past four you have been at a desk. And never once did you do courier work. Besides that, you have a genuine medical condition that is a prerequisite for this particular job of work. The Opposition knows about that injury you suffered too. You have quite a lot of pain, don't you?'

Dawes was surprised. Never before had the Old Man mentioned his injuries or hinted that he even knew any details of them. He managed to grunt assent.

'Doctor Mortensen sees you regularly for therapy and medication.' Axe sucked on his pipe. 'He suggests a sea voyage. For your health.'

Dawes jerked upright, despite the blandishments of the chair. 'A cruise? Where? What vessel?' He found himself interested, for sun and rest were the only things that gave him any real relief from his chronic pain. At his desk job, with its lower pay, he couldn't afford much time for those.

He didn't notice that he hadn't asked what the job might be, but Axe quirked an eyebrow. Dawes felt himself grow hot with embarrassment.

The Old Man seemed not to notice. He relit his pipe for the third time and pointed its stem at Dawes.

'The *Victorine* is a cruise ship ostensibly belonging to a European consortium, operating under Liberian registration. Actually it belongs to a family associated closely with the Brokers.'

Dawes perked up his ears. 'We're investigating that bunch, then?'

'Not in this case. No, we have a sleeper in Libya who is bringing out some ticklish information about terrorist activities in the Middle East. He'll board the *Victorine* at Marseilles as a steward, replacing one who is resigning because of family problems. Mahmoud couldn't manage the transfer of information in France, because he's being watched by one of the terrorist groups.

'He had already arranged to replace the steward. The charter for the *Victorine* is a cruise designed for elderly invalids, complete with doctors, nurses, complete hospital suite. Everything for the wealthy traveller who can't manage normal travel arrangements. There he should make the drop without risk and go on to Libya, where he will rejoin his family.'

'And I am to become an elderly invalid?' Dawes knew his tone was acid, but it was too late to change it.

Axe grinned and offered him the cigarette box. Dawes waved it aside. 'Don't go all coy with me. You want me because I can qualify as a passenger on this cruise. What, exactly, is this all about?'

'Just what I say. Several prominent physicians have decided to sponsor this on behalf of elderly or otherwise incapacitated patients who love and want to travel. It's by way of being an experiment, with others to follow if it works well. The cruise will start in New York on June eleventh. Additional passengers will join at Southampton on the twentieth. The French contingent will join the ship at Marseilles on July second.'

'Why such long gaps?'

'It's going to be a most leisurely cruise, stopping along the way anywhere there are points of interest. Those able will go ashore for tours and visits to special places. The others can sit on deck and see the countryside. All under the eyes of several exceptional doctors.'

'So the French bunch will get short-changed.'

Axe frowned. 'Americans cross the Atlantic west to east, go around the coast to the Med, taking in all the sights along the European and African coasts. They go back home again, and the French from Marseilles do the Med cruise, go across the Atlantic east to west, cruise along the shore of the U.S., then go home again. At least, that's the way the promoters are planning it.'

Dawes nodded. 'Everyone, I predict, is going to make pots of money. Sounds like a natural. I can't say I like being a crippled ancient, though. I assume you have Mortensen primed to give me the necessary credentials.'

'Mortensen is one of the sponsors. He jumped at the chance to send you off on a long R-and-R. He told me you've been working too hard and resting too little and he didn't care why I wanted you to go along.'

Dawes was not surprised that the plans were all made before consulting him. When had he ever refused an assignment?

'So how long should I plan to be gone? Two months?'

'Make it three,' Axe suggested. You can afford it, for you'll get hazard pay. Not that there's any hazard attached to this one, but those are the rules. When you're assigned outside the country on secret work, you get extra. Don't pack, by the way. We're going to spring for an entire wardrobe suitable to a man of your wealth and position.'

'Which is who and what?' he asked. 'Retired gangster? Scion of a wealthy family?'

'Oil,' said the Old Man with admirable brevity. 'You're a petroleum engineer who struck it rich wildcatting in Texas and made your bundle before the oil slump. You were injured in an air crash four years ago, and aren't making a very good recovery. Anyone hearing your name will recognize it. You even look something like the real Stephen David Stokes. All the information is in your packet.'

'And if I run into the real Stokes and he asks me why I'm pretending to be him?' Dawes asked.

'You won't. He is — was — one of us. He's gone, without a trace that we can find. When you've finished with his identity, he'll disappear officially. In seven years, his heirs will inherit.'

Dawes felt a sinking sensation. He never could get used to losing people, which was another reason why he liked his desk job more than he ever would have believed.

He glanced at the Old Man. 'Would it be all right if I asked for a pair of alligator shoes? I know they're endangered, but I have always wanted a pair, ever since I was a boy.'

'Also a pair of snakeskin cowboy boots,' Axe agreed 'Nothing's too good for our Stokes. Not to mention our Dawes.'

It was the nearest thing to something personal that Dawes had ever heard from the Old Man. That told him something about his position in the agency, as well as the lack of danger in this present assignment. But he was too old a hand to think that any job at all was totally risk-free or went just as expected.

He flexed his leg. It hurt like hell.

6

Harley Street
London
8 May

Dear Benjamin,

You may recall that I have mentioned a cruise as part of your treatment. The physicians' group with which I have corresponded has arranged a special expedition that should suit you eminently well, and I have put your name on their list. You will embark 20th June from Southampton.

I am pausing while you pour yourself the whisky-and-water that I have expressly forbidden and to allow you to exhaust your formidable store of expletives. I know you altogether too well. But do not, I beg, sit down and dash off a curt note of refusal.

Your Division has sanctioned this (I understand that you are officially retired. I also understand the reality of your position). Since you have actually retired from the political scene, the Division is your only excuse for refusing to take this trip that may well restore some of your vigour.

C. assures me that he has written you, and his missive should arrive in the same post with this one. I even have a private nod from H.R.H.

All urge you to take this time of rest, to relax from your labours, and to enjoy this most unusual opportunity.

I will not deny that your age has something to do with my decision to insist, but admit it or not, you are growing older. Do sit for an hour and think about this opportunity.

Thinking always soothes your disposition, as I can attest.

Then write to confirm that you will go.

Warmest regards,
Hugh Weathering

★　★　★

Dear Hugh . . . or should I be properly humble and address you as Doctor Weathering — ?

As you may suspect, I have used some colourful language, as you prescribed. I have read a bit of Catullus to calm my temper. I have fumed and sputtered, furious at your reference to my age. Yet I have come, at last, to a recognition that you are in the right.

When I visited you in March it was not because I thought I needed a general checkup. It was because I have lacked energy for too long. I felt, to be honest, perfectly rotten, and I feel no better now.

Though my contribution to the Division is now solely advisory, I find that my judgment seems to be suffering along with my health. So, though I do not admit for a moment that your cruise will put me back into fine fettle, I will undertake it, simply because I know you believe that it will.

You are, after all, the physician. I am only an old warhorse with no war left in me.

Who would have thought, when we were together at Eton, that you would be ordering me about in this fashion?

Your disgruntled patient,
Benjamin Scarlatt

*   *   *

Whitehall
8 May

Benjamin Scarlatt
The Hollies, Hants.

Dear Benjamin,

Weathering tells me that you are in need of a good rest.

I have noted of late that you seem not quite up to par, and I second his recommendation. Take advantage of the opportunity he has arranged, for we are in the doldrums at the moment. Your help and advice can be spared for the present.

Go, and come back refreshed.

Challoner

★　★　★

The Hollies
10 May

Sir Archibald Challoner
Whitehall

Dear Archie,

I surrender! I shall go, of course, but I do not agree to like it. When I return, I expect to find a fine muddle in the Ministry, as usual. Still, if you are willing to risk the inevitable, then on your own head be it.

With resignation,
Benjamin Scarlatt

★　★　★

MEMO TO RENTAL AGENT:
The Hollies will be available for let, furnished, for two months, beginning

20 June. Usual terms apply.
Scarlatt

* * *

MEMO TO KENNEL:
The two terriers will be delivered for boarding on 20 June. Special treatment, as usual. In the event of emergency, inform Persiphal, Lynch, and Beene, Chancery Lane, London.

* * *

12 May

My dearest Louise,
You will be surprised to hear from me, knowing what a rotten correspondent I have been. I am, however, doing something that will certainly astonish you — not voluntarily, I might add. I am about to embark upon a recreational cruise.

I pause to allow you to regain your composure. I even suspect what your thoughts may be: 'What? My father, taking a cruise? Taking time away from his principal interest in life? The world is about to end with a solid explosion!'

Near enough?

While I am not nearly as decrepit as my physician and Challoner seem to think, I am nearing sixty-eight years of age. It has occurred to me that life is uncertain at any age and most especially after one passes sixty. If something should happen while I am taking that accursed voyage, I would like to recall that I have taken the time to let you know how very satisfactory a daughter you have been to me.

Your mother, bless her, would be proud to know how well you have cared for me, when I would allow it. I am also delighted with your choice of a husband and your methods with my grandchildren. I have never said so, I suppose, but I feel the time has come.

Should any mishap occur, you will of course hear from my solicitors.

I have arranged my estate in such a manner as to give you both security and freedom of mind. I know you are protesting silently as you read this, for monetary considerations have never been of much importance to either of us. Yet I understand what a bother such matters can be in times of stress. I hope I have saved you from the possibility of worry in the midst of sorrow.

Let me assure you that I have no premonitions of mortality. Other, of course, than those I always entertain when forced to do something I particularly dislike doing.

I feel as well as I have for some time, and I expect to be totally bored for two months and several odd days.

I shall be, you must understand, surrounded by elderly crocks.

Wealthy, elderly crocks. Do you realize the dimensions of this catastrophe?

If I should succumb, it will be to ennui, I am certain.

I do expect to greet you in August. If I am not in the pink of health, you may lay that at the door of Hugh Weathering.

Until then I remain . . .

Your loving Father

* * *

MEMO TO PERSIPHAL, LYNCH, AND BEENE:

I have signed the codicil to my Will, and it is enclosed herewith. I assume that my affairs are now in order. If not, inform me before mid-June.

Benjamin Scarlatt

7

Olive hated driving. Her short neck got tired and ached. Her short arms cramped and went stiff, and her short temper was better left unmentioned. She'd decided long ago that automobiles were built for six-footers with steel spines, not for elderly ladies whose inches didn't equal their needs.

This new task demanded a very long drive. Kelvin, Texas, was not served by trains, planes, or even convenient buses. It lay almost off the edge of the map, in the middle of the pine forests of East Texas, and a car was the only method for getting there on time.

She glanced aside at her knitting bag, which held other things than knitting. The Dictator had a skilful corps of bodyguards, and they would be uneasy here in such alien territory. Inside the bag was her victim's itinerary, and she blessed the whim that took him to visit his old

65

teacher from mission school, who had worked in colonial Africa.

The flash of a tail-light in the dusk ahead warned Olive of some obstruction, and she slowed on the hill. The road was a winding one, ducking and dipping over abrupt hills. It was narrow and ill paved, and you could seldom see what lay ahead until you were on top of it. She slowed still more, watching two cars that were pulled to a halt in her lane. Men stood in the road, waving flashlights.

State police?

Her internal alarms went off, but silently.

She braked to a stop, then crawled forward, following the car that was being motioned off the main road and into a lane. A man with a light stopped her at the gate. He was armed; even in the dim light she recognized the shape of an Uzi.

The man bent down to the window, and she clasped her left hand to her heart. The sharp blade in her bra was ready to her fingers that way.

'Officer?' she quavered, 'is there something wrong?'

His shoulders relaxed, and his entire stance became less wary as he surveyed her in the light of the flash. 'We're looking for escaped convicts. Everyone must stop and have their cars searched. Pull into that field, behind the Ford, and go into the old school house there, will you, Ma'am?'

She nodded. 'Of course. My, how exciting!'

A tough, middle-aged woman armed with another Uzi met her in the field as she emerged from the car. 'In there,' she snapped, pointing toward the dark building.

Olive reached for her purse and knitting bag. Before she could get them, the woman said, 'No luggage. Go!'

'Will it take long?' Olive sounded frightened and subdued.

There was grim amusement in the woman's voice. 'No. Not long.' She jerked her weapon toward the building. 'Now go.'

Olive doddered toward the school house behind the overgrown trees. She could hear mutters and coughs inside, as she entered the black doorway. A wail told her that at least one child had been caught up in the dragnet.

Fumbling her way along the wall, she found a bench and sat, thinking hard. Those were certainly not officers of the law. She'd been here before, and even in East Texas things were not done this way. These people were armed with the wrong weapons as well. They had to be terrorists of some stripe, she felt certain.

She had just been taken hostage, she was convinced, and she chuckled silently. Her captors would find they had caught a fish they didn't know how to handle.

There was a disturbance at the door as someone entered with a flashlight and played it across the line of startled faces. Five white faces, two adult black faces, two pale children, an infant. Eleven hostages, counting herself.

She couldn't see those behind the light, as a man's voice barked, 'You must now sit quietly and wait. You are prisoners of the International Justice League, and you will be held hostage until our demands are met. We will not hesitate to kill anyone who makes any disturbance or problem of any kind.'

Olive wondered how many there might be in the group. She had counted three men in the road, the woman in the field. There would be at least one other, acting as liaison with whomever they intended to contact. If she considered the total number to be eight, she probably wouldn't miss it by much, she thought. Even armed as they were, she suspected that she could handle the situation without innocent bloodshed.

The man said, 'Gretta will be in charge. Ask her before you move from your place. The john is behind the door over there. Do not try anything with Gretta. She is not a patient person.'

'Right.' That was the woman's voice. She came forward from behind the speaker into the light and gestured toward one of the men on the bench. He stumbled toward her, and she handed him a Coleman lantern, which she proceeded to light.

'Hang that on the hook up there on the wall.'

The lantern sputtered, then steadied. When it was in place, Olive could see that the old school house had been roughly but efficiently blacked out. Another lantern was placed on the other side of the room; in their harsh glare, Gretta had a clear view of her charges.

The Knit Lady settled herself on her bench as comfortably as possible. Her hands trembled in her lap, and her lips quivered artistically. She longed for her knitting, for the steady rhythm of the needles, the pulling of the wool through her fingers was soothing. Her needles were also peerless weapons, but now she didn't have her normal tools of the trade to depend upon.

If worse came to worst, she could kill with her bare hands, small and arthritic though they were, thanks to the Group. But she was glad of the scalpel, cold and hard against her wrinkled chest, its blade protected by a slip of plastic.

She leaned back against the rough wall and closed her eyes. What had terrorists found of interest near Kelvin, Texas? It was of no commercial or political importance.

There were no prisons worthy of the name. Only one thing had brought her here, and that had to be what brought these people, as well.

Balfour G'dami. The atrocities his dictatorship caused had brought about her contract, she was sure. Only the fact that he had always been rabidly anti-Communist had given him clout with the State Department, allowing him to visit the U.S. to beg for money to fight the insurgents in Upper Balvi. That done, he was going home via Texas to visit his former teacher.

She remembered the publicity, just before he set off on this journey, about the prisoners he had tortured to death. Probably, these people were allies of those counter-revolutionaries, trying to pull their fellows loose by the use of hostages. While G'dami wouldn't care a fig for American citizens, he had to watch his step, for Congress had not yet approved his grant.

That was a usable hypothesis, right or wrong. Anyone who had not taken intense interest in G'dami's whereabouts would not have known he was in this part of the country. His itinerary had been classified, and he was supposed to be in Washington until the end of the week. The secrecy surrounding this side trip was the only thing allowing her a good chance to fulfill her contract.

With his weapons grant still hanging in the balance, G'dami would be forced to play ball with the terrorists, if she had read the situation correctly. She smiled. It wasn't nearly as hard to come and go without a trace now, with the track muddied by the presence of these gorillas. What she must do would be blamed on them.

Olive relaxed and tried to rest. In the harsh light of the lanterns, the children had stopped fretting and were sleeping, stretched along the benches behind their parents. The adults tried talking once, but Gretta's glare reduced them to silence. The Knit Lady watched them all with the patience of a tiger at a waterhole.

She closed her eyes at last, though she didn't remove her glasses. Her breathing deepened to a steady rhythm, punctuated by delicate little snorts. Gretta watched her charges for a long time, and when it seemed everyone was asleep, she rose from her chair and slipped silently out of the door. The lock clicked behind her.

Olive opened one eye. All those near seemed to be soundly asleep. She rose and moved noiselessly to a window and put her ear against the fabric covering the glass.

' . . . now. It's secure here. You and Garek and Chess can handle any problem this bunch of sheep might manage. We should be in town when Oscar makes the demand. We might need to make a show of force.'

Gretta's quiet reply was inaudible, but it was followed by footsteps drawing away from the building. Olive slipped into her place again and closed her eyes.

A car engine came to life in the middle distance. Gretta unlocked the door and reentered the room.

An hour passed. Olive feigned deep sleep. But at last she moaned, moving restlessly. Her hands convulsed in her lap and rose to her chest. She gasped, pressing her fingers against her heart.

'Ohhhh,' moaned the Knit Lady.

'Shut up! Shut up!' Gretta whispered. She cat-footed over to bend above the old woman. 'What's the matter?'

'Heart . . . ' gasped the Knit Lady.

'Oh, damn!' grunted the woman, bending still lower, her weapon loose in her hand.

Olive cut her throat smoothly and dumped her to one side, missing the spurt of blood from the severed jugular. The Uzi fitted solidly into her hand.

'And then there were two,' breathed Olive Rienzi.

A young woman on the next bench shifted in her sleep. The old woman froze until she settled down again, and then moved to turn out both lanterns before approaching the window again. She climbed onto the unoccupied bench beneath the opening and pulled away the black cloth covering it. Her knee was aching fiercely, but she ignored it and peered out into the night.

One man stood beside the corner of the building. She could see the tip of his cigarette glowing, but she couldn't spot the other guard who should be there. Creeping to the door, Olive picked the lock with one of her old-fashioned wire hairpins.

The hinges had been newly oiled, and the door opened silently; she grabbed a handful of gravel from the path and flung it toward the area just beyond the window she had used before. Almost before the pebbles hit the ground, she was again on the bench.

The red coal of the cigarette hit the ground. Two sets of running steps converged upon the area where the gravel fell. Two shapes bulked against the slightly paler sky.

The Uzi spoke in one short, efficient burst.

There came a babble of confused questions and answers in the room as the sleepers woke, confused. Olive was out of the door before anyone knew what had happened or thought of striking a match. Her car started easily and quietly, and she headed again toward Kelvin.

The tiny hamlet was silent, the single traffic light blinking amber. The click of the blinker seemed loud in the silence. Three streetlights stood along the block-long main street, and Olive avoided it, turning into Carpenter Street when she saw the sign. She had memorized her map in complete detail.

She turned right off Carpenter onto Maidstone. Dead end at Seeley, with a left turn. Three houses down — but she didn't drive onto Maidstone. She parked the car in front of a dark house and walked the few blocks to the missionary's small home. She had been informed that G'dami was staying there, as Kelvin had no hotel.

The map was dead on: the alley that cut between Maidstone and Seeley was marked, even the adjacent garages and lawns being identified. She went steadily past the back yard marked as having an above-ground swimming pool and the garage with a trellis of roses running up it. There was the parked motorboat on its trailer.

Then she was against the board fence, looking through its gaps into the neat back lawn of Jonathan Latimer. His daughter was G'dami's former teacher.

Olive took from her pocket a pencil flashlight and tied a red handkerchief over its bulb, dimming the glow-worm glimmer to the barest of illumination. Even then she only switched it on when she sensed she was approaching some obstacle.

Now she was across the lawn, against the rear wall of the house. There were three windows to her right — according to her map, that was the room where G'dami would sleep. The guest room. As she tensed to move, a dog began barking, seeming almost on top of her. Then she realized it was inside the house, and at some distance.

Ducking beneath the level of the windows, she scooted to the corner and looked toward the street. A black car idled there, its tail-light casting a red glow onto the gravel.

Aha! Oscar must be arriving to make his pitch.

Now there was movement inside the house. Lights went on, and there was a low babble of talk. She took the opportunity to risk one eye above the level of the windowsill of the guest room.

Light from another room illuminated the one into which she looked enough to let her see fairly clearly. The bed was right up against the window, and she could see the silhouette of a burly man dark against the dim light.

There was a rumble of talk in a language she didn't understand. Three men stood between the bed and the door, weapons drawn, while a fourth called from the front of the house.

The dog was making so much noise that the sound of her Uzi was lost in the uproar. G'dami toppled sideways onto the bed. The other three men wilted onto the floor. Olive was out of the yard and up the alley before anyone touched the light switch to see what had happened in that room.

* * *

Again her car slid through silent streets. The sound of a siren in the distance gave her time to park in front of a sleeping house and slip down so the car looked empty, parked for the night. A three-year-old Chevy with a detachable flasher on its roof tore past as she waited, and she watched it out of sight through the rear window.

In thirty minutes she was in another county. Within two hours she was on a bus to Dallas, the car safely delivered to her contact in Nacogdoches. At dawn she was waiting for her plane, and by lunchtime she was again snugly ensconced in her own apartment.

Nobody had seen her. Not really. She was a dumpy shape, an elderly woman, not worth a second glance. The people in the school house hadn't had an opportunity to look at her, and, concerned with their own danger, they probably wouldn't have anyway.

She went out after the afternoon papers. The headlines were most satisfactory.

G'DAMI ASSASSINATED
BALVIAN PREMIER KILLED IN GUN
    BATTLE
TERRORIST ATTACK CLAIMS G'DAMI

The terrorists had played into her hands. With a bunch of hostages telling confused stories about their capture, who would ever think to blame anyone else for her completed assignment?

Smiling, the Knit Lady began making out her bill for expenses. Unlike others in her profession, she delivered first and then asked for payment. That left her free to follow her conscience, as well as to keep her independence.

No employer would dare try to renege on his obligation, she knew. She was a weapon that could aim itself. One who went back on his word would die, and everyone was beginning to understand that.

8

It didn't take Dawes much time to set his affairs in order before his prolonged absence. He did quite a lot of his preliminary arrangement on his way home from Axe's townhouse, stopping at the office where his apartment complex was managed and paying three months rent in advance. He also paused at a florist's shop and ordered flowers to be delivered to both his sisters on the anniversary of their mother's death.

He detoured by the 'repair shop' that fronted for the Agency and cleared out his desk. That brought a lot of questions from the secretaries and his two associates, neither of whom was able to repair a broken shoelace, much less an inoperable TV.

He gave them the story he had cooked up with Axe, which was almost true. He'd found that the best way to lie: make it mostly true and any discrepancy could be attributed to a lapse of memory.

'Look, I'm not dying or anything,' he said to Amy. 'I'm still having trouble with my leg. This spring has given me fits, as you may have noticed every time. I howled like a banshee when I bumped my knee on the desk. The doctor thinks I should take some time off. That's absolutely all. I can't afford it, but the boss is in a flap and is going to carry on with my pay, so what can I do?'

He didn't mention a cruise. He had never told anyone who his doctor was, wasn't sure if any of them had an idea in the world who their 'boss' was, either.

'The boss says to take off three months. Any other outfit would fire me if I mentioned such a thing. But he's told me to go to a warm climate and rest for the entire time. I'm even getting to catch up on years of back sick leave. I just hope you hotshots won't have stolen my job when I get back.'

'You're sure you're not just trying to keep us from worrying?' Gail asked. She rubbed the bridge of her nose, a sure sign she suspected he might be lying.

'You want a note from my doctor, Teacher?'

She laughed. 'You take care of yourself, anyway. I don't want to have to break in another manager. You were hard enough to deal with.'

Amy giggled. She could recognize teasing, if you gave her a couple of minutes to catch on. 'It's too bad you didn't let us know. We could have given you a party.'

Kim suspected that Amy's idea of Heaven was one vast alcoholic party, with God playing a clown and wearing a lamp shade on his head. He had hoped for years that she wasn't as dimwitted as she appeared to be. But her work was done quickly and accurately. He suspected she might be one of their seldom-used 'sleepers.'

Garwood and Haines were noncommittal, but he could see the speculation in their guarded eyes. Both were working toward time in the field, training all the while. Both showed promise, although Haines was brighter and more flexible.

Dawes knew both were hoping his

assignment, whatever it might be, would remove him as an obstacle to their upward movement. It was nothing personal. He had felt the same, in his own salad days. He smiled at both, took the flight bag into which he had packed his personal items, and said, 'Keep it warm, boys. I'll be back in the fall. Without fail.'

When he was out on the street he allowed himself to smile. Had he ever been so easy to read?

From force of habit, he took a roundabout way in approaching his apartment building: Through a service alley, up the interior fire stairs, outside at the end of the corridor on the third floor, onto the exterior fire escape, climbing it to his bedroom window. It had been four years since he had done that. Something about going back on active duty had reactivated his old instincts.

On the platform outside his window, he set down his bag and briefcase and reached for the hidden latch he had installed to let himself in, at need. He had used it twice, both times when he lost a key.

Even as he reached toward the latch, something warned him and he dropped flat. A slug sang over his head from inside the room, to splat on the brick wall across the alley behind him. Once he was down he didn't move. Let his attacker think he was dead!

Someone came to the window and stared out. He could feel that gaze slide along his back and he thought for a moment that the assassin was coming out. But in a minute he heard steps moving away. The cool bastard was going out into the corridor. That silenced automatic would rouse no interest; unfortunately, shattering glass wasn't unusual in any neighbourhood, these days.

Dawes didn't change his position, though he slid a hand along his side to palm the miniature automatic from its concealed holster at his belt. Face down, he looked through the grille into the alley below. His would-be killer would be checking further before he left, or he didn't know his business.

A shoe sole grated on the dirty

pavement below. X was going to look up from beneath and probably shoot him again, just to make sure. A foot came into view. The top of a sleek head.

'Damn,' Dawes breathed. 'Scalpel. Now who in hell has he sold out to? And how has he fooled Axe?'

The foreshortened figure was under him now. Dawes breathed shallowly, remaining motionless. A wedge of pale face turned up, studying him. The weighted last leg of the ladder was some ten feet above the pavement, and he felt that Scalpel wouldn't trouble himself to hook it down, even if he found something that would do the job.

No, Skelley would shoot him again, several times. Dawes eased the little gun into position without any betraying quiver and fired once. Scalpel's face jerked, and a dot of red appeared between his slanting eyebrows.

In the alley space, the noise of the shot was deafening. Before it died away, Dawes was inside his apartment with the window shut and the blinds drawn to hide the broken glass.

He dialled Axe's number.

'Yes?' The man sounded relaxed and sleepy.

'We have been talking for several minutes. Please look at your watch.'

'Right.' Axe was quick on the uptake. 'You called at four-ten to set up an appointment for this afternoon. Six o'clock, correct?'

'Yes,' Dawes said. 'You may need to remember that.'

Sirens screamed in the street, drawing nearer. Drillbit brushed his suit and his bags, smoothed his hair, and went out into the hall. He went down the interior service stairs and was out of the rear door before any confusion had begun to build at its front.

He didn't go to the parking garage three blocks away. Instead of taking his own car he walked a few blocks and caught a cab. The sun was low when he ran up the townhouse steps, ignoring the misery in his leg.

Axe opened the door. 'Scalpel is out.' His tone was strange, almost as if he felt some foreshadowing of trouble.

'He won't be back. I shot him about thirty minutes ago,' Dawes said.

'Hmmm . . . interesting. Come into the study, and Maude will make tea.'

Dawes grinned. Any unseen listener might think Maude a housekeeper, ready to make a guest welcome. But Dawes knew that if there was tea Maude would not make it. She kept her neat head bent over computer terminals, code manuals, and reports from agents in the field. She could make sense of the most confusing set of circumstances.

He took three minutes to make his report. Axe watched his face, but Maude stared at the wall, and he could almost see her wheels turning. At last she turned to her terminal and began tapping away.

Figures, diagrams, and words began to chase each other across the screen. Dawes tried to decipher the thing, but he was getting near-sighted as well as lame.

Axe didn't bother. That was Maude's task. When she pushed her chair back, the Old Man looked at her inquiringly.

'There was a rumour last week that we might possibly have a leak here at headquarters. We'd had two narrow squeaks that weren't normal. I checked superficially, but nothing showed up on the files.

'I've had Internal Security checking it out in depth, but they haven't reported anything. If it was Scalpel all the while, he could have been covering his tracks via computer all the time.' She pushed her glasses up her nose and stared at Dawes, her grey eyes wide.

'But why? And for whom?'

Axe turned his pipe stem in his fingers. 'By now he may have informed his principals that Dawes is on another job. He might even have found a way to break your supercode, Maude, and told them about the cruise. Scalpel was sharp, you can't deny that.'

He stared out the window into the calm green garden. 'This may not be quite the rest cure I'd planned for you after all, Dawes. We have no way to warn our man. You just have to follow through and hope for the best.'

Dawes felt an insane desire to grin. He'd hoped all along that things would turn out to be more exciting than they promised to.

Something inside him craved the old game, the adrenaline rushes, the tight corners. He was back in the game. He felt his smile escaping his control, and he found Axe smiling back at him with complete understanding. They were, after all, professionals, and understood each other perfectly.

'So when do I go?' he asked.

9

Gianello sat before the fire in his study. Although it was late May, his bones craved heat, though he knew his associates sweltered. Even his employees dreaded coming here to get their orders, but that was their problem. He enjoyed seeing them sweat physically as well as emotionally.

When Hitchman knocked, he grunted an affirmative and swiveled his leather chair to face the man. Hitchman was sweating already, and Gianello smiled.

'We've made contact,' the leg-man said. 'Through Genno. It's just as well we used him as a reference — the Knit Lady isn't taking on new jobs that aren't rock ribbed and copper-bottomed. Even Genno had to provide a lot of assurances, he told me.'

'So?'

'She agreed to go abroad for us, at our expense, and for a pretty steep fee. She already has a passport under some name she used for a job. We won't need to fix that up, which will save some time and money.'

Gianello tapped the end of his gold ballpoint against his thumbnail. 'Has Tomassini's pet doctor made the arrangements?'

'No problem. Tomassini has him well trained.'

'Then get the word out to Binh. They'll need time to get their act together on the European end of things. We'll stash Scarlatt, once we have our hands on him, at the villa on Corsica. Make sure there's a doctor there. He's an old guy and we don't want him dying on us. They'll want proof he's alive more than once, if I know the British.

'Dead, he's just so much meat. Alive, he's the key to our entire British operation. You make sure Binh understands that.' He glared at Hitchman until the man squirmed.

'Any slip-up, any accidental fatality and their tails will be in a sling. I'll put every man I have out after their necks, if they mess up on this.' He frowned ferociously.

Hitchman's forehead was greasy with

sweat. He looked both awed and frightened, which was just the effect Gianello intended. If Hitch was scared shitless when he made contact with Binh, he'd succeed in frightening Binh. That was what made the Brokers' organization work — failure was punished with death, and everyone knew it.

When the door closed behind Hitchman, Gianello leaned back in the vast leather chair, his subtle mind already shifting pawns on the invisible chessboard that was his plotting. All the elements of the game were now moving into position. Now it all depended upon the disposition of Benjamin Scarlatt — if he made that journey, all would be well.

The old man knew Scarlatt — had known him for much longer than anyone suspected. He, too, had been involved in the War, though not officially or with the sanction of any government. An obscure young man from an even more obscure Sardinian village, he'd had an eye for opportunity. He had milked the War for all it was worth, without risking his neck much at all.

He had a good deal going with the

Nazis, slipping them crucial messages about the various resistance movements or the transfer of Allied airmen being smuggled into neutral territory.

He had done a modest amount of gun-running to those same resistance people as well, though they hadn't enough money to make it very attractive. The guns kept him in touch with them, however, which led to much larger payments from the Nazis.

For him, it was a profitable war. Stashing his gains in Switzerland, he had been about to retire from action when Scarlatt tumbled to his operation and put him out of business, almost catching him in the process. He owed Scarlatt for that, and Gianello never forgot a debt of any kind.

Although he had not hinted as much to his associates, he had no intention of allowing Scarlatt to survive his abduction, once their goal was achieved. He had arranged for other orders to reach the Knit Lady containing instructions nobody would ever know about except for himself and that enigmatic assassin.

Gianello sighed and swiveled his chair to gaze out of the window. He was surprised at Al Genno. The man seemed to believe that this hit-man would refuse an assignment because of conscience. That was foolish.

He had known hit-men all his life. They were a strange breed without real human emotion. They did what they were paid to do and never questioned their orders.

This one would do the same.

He wondered what ulterior motive Genno might have for putting about such an obviously ridiculous story.

10

The Hollies
May 20

Sir Archibald Challoner
Whitehall

Dear Archie,

I have been thinking, while packing up my possessions and getting myself ready for this triple-damned cruise, about the rumour we picked up earlier in the spring. I have wondered for some time if there might be some organization of the shady sort infiltrating our shipping industry, and I am now almost certain.

Enclosed you will find a packet of papers containing the fruits of my cerebration. It should give you food for thought, while I am away. Read it over and see what you can derive from it. There are some people in the Ministry at this moment who are not behaving in quite the normal manner.

Others, up and down the chain of bureaucracy, are also not reacting quite as usual. I suspect some multinational criminal organization is attempting in-depth penetration of our system. Though smuggling is a likely part of their intent, drug-running is almost certainly a large factor.

Sniff around. Get Leverett to put his famous instincts to work.

I shall think with pleasure of you, rummaging about in stuffy offices filled with musty files, while I watch blue waters and green millionaires from the deck of a cruise ship.

Regards,
Ben

Postscript: I also have a strange feeling about this cruise. Perhaps it is only because I hate the idea of being old and ill enough to be forced to set out upon it.

B.

11

Olive found the cruise amazingly enjoyable. She had never in her life taken a vacation of any kind, for she and Francesco had been forced to work hard every minute in order to survive. They had loved their quiet life, but it had never occurred to her that there was more to see and do in the world than they managed to find together.

Now she had more money than she had ever hoped to possess. She was untroubled by any thought of business left undone at home, and she could rest her aching bones in the sun and watch people. Even a short bout of seasickness two days out didn't last, and it gave her a yardstick by which to measure the joy of getting over it.

Before Francesco's death, if such an opportunity to travel had come her way she would have approached it warily, suspicious of such good fortune. Now she let herself relax into her role, feeling her way into relationships with the people around her.

At first the task she was assigned had seemed relatively harmless and simple. When Genno guaranteed the bona fides of the organization wanting her services, she had accepted his word. Yet that did not mean she was naively trusting. Both she and Genno understood, without a word spoken, that she provided insurance for herself, whatever the situation. Information was in unguessable hands, to be sent to the proper authorities if she died in any suspicious manner.

Of course she did not know the identity of her employer. She didn't want to know, in most cases, but this job seemed innocuous enough. Make a confidant of an elderly Englishman. Sedate him at the proper time and see that he fell, unharmed, into the right hands. She agreed to that without hesitation. When her instructions arrived, however, she found attached to the original document a handwritten note. Genno had explained to this person, she knew, her methods and her limits. The arrogant bastard took it for granted that she was a two-bit hired gun with no conscience. He wanted her to accompany Scarlatt to his place of confinement and to kill him, once the word came down that the desired result was achieved.

Olive knew what was happening between nations and other power-brokers. Benjamin Scarlatt was a name she knew, and he was a man still needed in the world. She'd be damned if she'd kill him, and she was certainly not going to connive at his abduction, if he impressed her in person as the kind she thought he must be. She would get to know him, that was a foregone conclusion. That way, she would be at hand if a secondary conspirator might be on hand to take up the work if she failed.

As she knitted or played rummy in the lounge with other elderly women, she found herself watching her fellows and even the crew members with more than casual interest. Something was wrong. She could feel that among her companions were some who were not what they seemed, though she had not yet determined exactly who and why.

She could not, of course, get to know

everyone. The ship was large, with those on each deck chosen for compatible degrees of capability. They tended to associate with those on their own decks, and there were not the usual games and dances that might have mingled them more. Most were not physically able to do more than sit in the sun or, rarely, engage in a game of shuffleboard.

On Olive's deck, most were pretty well self-sufficient, though many groaned when rising from a chair or moved with some difficulty. She had feared she might be surrounded by senile incompetents, and she was pleased that she'd been wrong.

She found herself among a group whose bodies might be erratic, but whose minds were mostly keen, and whose senses of humor were still sharp and sometimes wicked. Most were about her own age, but Stephen Stokes was too young to feel quite at ease with his companions. She had noticed him at once, wondering if he might be one of those not-quites she had sensed.

The blue-haired contingent had tried

to recruit her for their daily knit and gossip sessions on the afterdeck, but she managed to evade them without being unfriendly. The younger woman in the wheelchair was different. Olive hoped to make friends with her, for something in her pale face and pain-haunted eyes reminded her of Francesco. However, Margaret Palfrey seemed too buried in her capsule of pain and unhappiness to pay much attention to those around her.

Olive arranged to sit next to her at meals and kept trying to break through her shell of silence, but it proved to be very hard going.

She had better luck with Stokes, who had a good sense of humour and a better sense of self preservation. It amused Olive that he used her as a sort of bodyguard to put off some of the harpies who shared their deck.

They talked sporadically, but neither seemed to be ill at ease when they fell silent. It was a comfortable relationship, and Olive decided that he must be what he said he was. She had no feeling of unease with him, as she had always felt with some of the bad hats she had met through the years.

She thought for a bit about him and Margaret Palfrey and came up with a brilliant plot. 'You need someone to keep off the biddies. Margaret needs someone to make her feel special. You should make up to her — tell her why, right up front, if you like. Though she isn't a bad-looking woman, not much older than you, I'd think, if you could see past her sickness.'

For a wonder, Stephen didn't object. Looking thoughtful, he said, 'I wonder why she was put on this deck instead of down with the ones in wheelchairs.'

'I wondered the same thing. Maybe her doctor felt it wouldn't be good psychologically to put her in with a bunch of very old and decrepit people. She needs to feel young, to be among people who are still able to enjoy life. It would be completely natural for you to seek her out. You're the youngest people on the boat, except for the crew.'

Stephen grinned. 'You're not the tough cookie I thought you were. You're nothing but a sentimental old matchmaker!'

Olive grunted. 'That's as may be. Probably not a woman breathes who doesn't have a bit of that in her someplace. But you think about what I said. It would be good for both of you, and at least you wouldn't have to refugee out behind me any more.'

Much to her surprise the young man followed her advice. Even more to her surprise, Margaret didn't welcome his attentions.

'What's the matter with that girl?' she asked Elizabeth Reed. 'She should be delighted to have a nice-looking young fellow like Stephen dancing attention. He may be a bit gimpy, but he's nice, and he has money. What more could she ask?'

Elizabeth gave a delicate snort. 'That young woman needs a good kick in the butt,' she said in her usual blunt way. 'Takes all her time and energy feeling sorry for herself, never noticing anything else. I'd like to dump her in the swimming pool, just to see if she had enough gumption to paddle out.'

Stephen joined Olive in their usual spot the next morning. 'You didn't have much luck,' she observed, needles clicking away. 'I gave you bad advice, I think.'

He stretched in his chair, hands clasped behind his head. 'It gave me something to do. I don't know — there's something about that lady. Something odd, but I can't put my finger on it.'

Olive nodded. 'Probably too much money all her life, never had to do anything she didn't want to do. Now she can't handle this thing that money can't buy her way out of. I've met a good few of those in my time.'

Stephen frowned slightly. 'I don't get the feeling that's the case. Have you ever noticed her hands? They're smooth now, but you can see she has worked hard. Her nails are warped, fingers broadened with stress. She's ashamed of them and keeps them hidden in her lap. She isn't what she seems, our Margaret Palfrey.'

Olive drew a deep breath, thinking hard. 'Come to think of it, she looks more Italian than English. Wouldn't you say Palfrey was English? Of course, she may be a widow. I don't really look like a Rienzi, now do I?'

He laughed. 'You look like Abie's Irish Rose,' he said.

'We have several people who don't look like their names,' she observed. 'Take the Goldfarbs. Neither looks Jewish.'

'And the Moreno-Estévezes.' he added. 'They look about as Spanish as you do.'

She laughed. 'Then there's the steward in my area, whose name, believe it or not, is Button Blivens. If he's not an Arab of some kind, I'll eat him. With hot sauce. There are a lot of the crew, do you realize, who are Middle-Easterners? I suppose with all the unrest there they jump at a chance to get jobs outside the area.'

Stephen's smile was rather odd. The feeling Olive had almost forgotten concerning him roused again. What on earth could there be about this nice young man that niggled at her sense of danger?

12

The leisurely voyage across the Atlantic ended at last, and Southampton harbour bustled about the *Victorine*. Olive spent a lot of time at the rail, watching the traffic and deciding whether to go ashore there. She had a hunch it might be better for her to remain on board while the others made the short excursions the doctors had arranged for their amusement.

Their passage up the Solent and her first sight of the Isle of Wight had her a bit dazzled. Those were names she had read in books, and to see the actual waters and the land itself delighted her.

She decided against the trip to the New Forest. She did, however, visit the Cherne Abbas giant, which she had seen in pictures and couldn't bear to miss.

When they returned from that jaunt, Benjamin Scarlatt had come aboard. In some esoteric manner, her employers had arranged that her cabin was only two doors down the same corridor from his.

Convenient.

He was also placed at the same table with her, sitting just beyond Margaret. Elizabeth was on his left, and Anthony Quayne rounded out the number, leaving one place waiting for a member of the French contingent.

Olive said little, that first evening, but she watched her prey unobtrusively. He was a big man, tall and solid, and she would have known from his bearing that he had spent part of his life in the military. When one of his tablemates asked a question, he answered politely, but it was clear to her that he was abstracted. Even Elizabeth's less than mannerly inquisitiveness dug nothing notable from him.

After dinner they all attended a movie, and Olive went too, simply to continue her observations. She had seen *The Sound of Music* too many times, so she found the darkened room useful for seeing without being observed. Scarlatt seemed relaxed, almost dozing during the movie.

The movie ended and the crowd straggled away to late games of bridge or to their rooms for the night. She managed to trip and drop her bag, spilling balls of red yarn and clattering needles all over the corridor outside her cabin.

'Do let me help you,' Scarlatt said, turning to assist her. They gathered up the things and returned them to the bag.

Then she grimaced and held up her hands. 'These things don't do what I tell them to, any longer.' The telltale swellings of arthritis marked her joints. 'They are the very devil. I hope you don't have that to contend with, Colonel Scarlatt.'

He handed her the knitting bag and smiled. 'I have every painful ailment the human body can fall heir to and a few invented solely for me,' he said.

She laughed and thanked him again, but she didn't try to extend the contact. Once inside her cabin, she thought about him, finding he was very much the gentleman she had expected him to be. She certainly would not kill him or even drug him, and that would mean she was about to be in just as much trouble in

109

Europe as she was in the United States.

'I simply will not act the Judas,' she said to her hairbrush. She laid it on the dressing table and looked into her own blue eyes in the mirror. 'I've done a good few things I'm not entirely proud of, but so far I can still look you in the eye without cringing,' she said to that other Olive.

'Somehow I don't think Francis would object seriously to anything I have done since he died. But this would be different. He would have liked Benjamin Scarlatt.' She tugged her grey hair onto the top of her head and secured it with a rubber band.

She lay awake for a long time, after turning out the light. Not only dissatisfaction with the assignment troubled her. Something about this entire cruise seemed strangely out of focus. On the surface it seemed a wonderful idea whose time had come. Yet there were people on this ship who did not fit their images. Button Blivens was not the only crew member who did not fit his name as well.

She turned on her side, sighed, and

turned back. At last she rose and put on jeans and a heavy black shirt. When she had one of her occasional sleepless nights, the only cure was to get up and walk off the mood that caused it. At home, that wasn't safe any more, but here on the ship it should be entirely so.

She moved silently up the corridor, her rubber soles useful for this more innocent purpose than they were usually called upon to serve. She stepped onto the deck, which was dimly lit by the ship's running lights. The ocean rolled like black oil alongside, as she leaned on the rail and looked outward into blackness.

The ship had never seemed so quiet. Though there were always tiny creaks and clatters and some deeper groans from the depths of the vessel, she had never been able to hear them clearly before.

Now the body of the ship at work spoke to her, and in some odd way it was comforting.

Olive started toward the spot where she usually had her deck chair, but the chairs were now stacked in their cubby and she didn't want to create a clatter. She moved

111

along the deck into shadows, where the lifeboat davit loomed against the stars. She perched herself on the deck and leaned against the metal frame, looking out to sea.

The ship talk, rivet to metal, wood to bolt, sank into the background of her thoughts. The immense quiet of the sea enclosed her, and she found herself relaxing at last, leaning more and more heavily against the davit. Braced as she was, even if she fell asleep, she knew she would not roll overboard. Better to find sleep here than to toss in her cabin.

Old reflexes brought her instantly awake. She didn't move, for something had waked her, something that was not a part of the working sounds of the ship or the night sounds of the water. She listened intently, not moving a muscle.

There! A whisper of rubber against wood . . . not shoes. Wheels? A faint squeal of metal on metal. That was a wheelchair, or she was not Olive Rienzi.

The night was not silent, but Olive's keen ears could make out the light breathing of the chair's occupant. What could Margaret be doing out here, alone and in the dark? There was only one answer.

She was waiting for someone.

The Knit Lady waited with the patience she had learned in a harder school than her teachers had created. Someone would come, or he would not. Either way, she would know, before returning to her bed.

* * *

He came so silently that his whisper almost made Olive jump.

'You were not seen?' It was a voice, even as a whisper, that Olive had noted carefully. No one using a name like Button Blivens could possibly escape her scrutiny.

'Of course not. I am no fool.' Margaret sounded weary, ill, almost desperate. What on earth could those two have in common?

Yet when they began to talk, softly and cautiously, it was in a tongue Olive did not understand. She almost cursed. She had learned Italian from Francesco and French from the nuns, long ago when she was a child. She could recognize German and even pick out a few familiar words. This was none of those languages. From the strange glottal and aspirate sounds, she thought it might be Arabic.

There was some kind of conspiracy going on right under her nose, and there was no way to learn what it might involve.

There were hundreds of wealthy people aboard the *Victorine*. Kidnapping might be a part of more schemes than the one that sent her here.

She wished that Axe were at the other end of that accommodation number, as he had been when she did tasks for the Agency. She needed a telephone at hand that could privately and unsuspiciously connect her with those who had both knowledge and power. She was, after all, old and alone, no matter how ruthless she might be in a pinch.

Olive was not about to use her special needlework on someone who might be innocent of any crime. This, strange as it might seem, might be a romantic assignation. But that grew less and less likely, as she listened to their voices. These were not the tender tones of love or lust but those more suited to a business meeting. Olive would have bet her last dime on it.

Smuggling? Possibly. Or any of a dozen other illegal, clandestine matters.

Their quiet mutter went on and on. Once Blivens seemed to be counting — there is a certain distinctive sound to the act of enumeration, even in an unknown tongue. Margaret spoke less frequently than the man did, but when she did it was in a commanding voice. She was obviously the superior, here.

They went quiet at last, and the wheels whispered away over the deck. Steps moved in the opposite direction, but Olive sat still in her place, thinking furiously. She must investigate this further. Somehow, she had to get through that shell of resistance that Margaret raised about herself. That was the first step.

The captain, if she approached him about this, would dismiss her as a doddering old fool and never think about it again. Until, perhaps, it was entirely too late to matter. No, she had to have more information.

She knew she needed help. She wondered briefly if Stephen Stokes might be up to the task. He was sound, she had decided very soon after meeting him. She sat beside him as he slept in his chair, dozing in the sun. He was a man in pain, as she recognized immediately. She had nursed Francesco too long to be fooled about that.

Still, even if he might not be up to much physically, he was bright and dependable. She felt that in her bones. She would keep him in mind, if she needed someone quickly.

Benjamin Scarlatt was tempting to think of, though he was much older than Stokes and must be ill to be here at all. Yet he had served through a couple of tough wars, trained for the hardest sort of service. Though he might not be up to a lot of rough and tumble, he might well know exactly what to do in almost any situation. If, that is, she could come up with some notion of what was in the wind.

She checked over the list of people on her deck with whom she had struck some acquaintance. Few seemed like possibilities for something shady. Juan Moreno-Estévez was large, true enough, and he looked as if he might have been a tough customer in years past. Now he watched people as closely as she did, but without her caution. He was also one of those she had that odd feeling about.

She listened for a long time for any sound of human presences on deck. Then she rose. First she must learn what she could about Margaret Palfrey. The woman herself was certainly not going to confide anything to her.

As much as she hated the idea, she knew she had to approach Al Genno. In this electronic age it wouldn't take long to receive a reply, and the codes Genno's organization had taught her allowed her messages to seem completely innocent.

In the morning she would write out a message and have it transmitted. Information was necessary, at this point.

13

Aboard the *Victorine*
June 28

Mrs. Pamela Grange
7009 Lily Court
Georgetown, VA

Dearest Pamela,

I am so grateful to you for insisting that I take this cruise, my dear. It has been interesting and restful, and my health seems much better. There are also many wonderful people. I have met Colonel Benjamin Scarlatt, who is the image of your British gentleman, and a tragic young woman, Margaret Palfrey, who is in a wheelchair and seems so depressed. I long to comfort her but cannot think how.

How is your mother? I worry about her health.

I do have some business that needs

your kind attention. Would you take the trouble to contact my lawyer and check on the status of the bonds he was to purchase for me? If he has not done so, do be sure to inform me as soon as possible. Cruises are all very well, but I cannot neglect my affairs. If I don't make certain of my assets, I may live to regret it. Do check with Jeffers and be sure he did as I requested.

Your help while I am away is most appreciated. Give my love to your dear mother.

Affectionately,
Olive Rienzi

Olive read the letter three times, making certain she had included all the information she needed to receive from Genno. It had taken all morning to work it into code, but she felt she had succeeded rather well. She handed the missive in at the purser's office and went to look for Margaret Palfrey.

She found the younger woman lying on her stomach on an air mattress, while her private nurse massaged her back and legs.

For once, Olive thought, she couldn't scoot away on rubber wheels when someone seemed likely to begin a conversation.

'Ah, Miss Palfrey! There's nothing like getting the circulation going to make you feel better. Are you seeing any improvement since you began the cruise? The sun and the rest, not to mention the food, have put me into fine shape . . . at least finer shape than I've been in for years.' She perched on a deck chair near the girl's head.

Glenda, the nurse, looked up and smiled. 'I believe the therapy is beginning to work. She moved her foot today, and that is the first indication of motion below her knees. One of these days she'll be up and about.' She rose and wiped the oil from her hands.

'Would you mind sitting with Margaret for a bit, Mrs. Rienzi? I have something I simply must do. It won't take fifteen minutes.'

When Olive nodded, she moved away, her tail of blond hair swinging above her neat bottom and long brown legs. The nurse's whites she wore did wonders for her tan.

Margaret had opened her mouth to protest, but the nurse was gone too quickly. She closed her lips and glanced sideways at Olive, who knew she was thinking there could be no danger in passing the time of day with an old lady who knitted. Olive reinforced the idea by taking out her knitting and beginning to work on another interminable red muffler.

'I have so wanted to get to know you, my dear,' she began in a grandmotherly tone. 'You seem so sad. I wish you would allow me to do something for you. Do you play bridge?'

Margaret shook her head, her dark hair ruffling in the breeze. Glints of gray caught the sunlight as she moved, though she seemed too young to have so much. 'Help me turn over,' she said gruffly.

Olive put down her knitting and caught the girl's shoulders, helping her to roll onto her back. One foot moved, trying to help, but the other trailed helplessly until Olive moved it into position.

'What happened to you?' Olive asked, resuming her place. 'A car wreck? I have so many friends who met disaster in that way. I have come to hate the automobile, for that reason.'

Margaret pulled a cushion and tucked it beneath her head to allow her to look more directly at her companion. 'No, not a car wreck.' The faint accent Olive had noticed from time to time seemed stronger than usual. 'This was done to me. Deliberately.'

Olive's expression of shock and amazement was only partly assumed as she dropped her knitting into her lap. 'But who? Why? I don't understand.'

The girl's smile was cruel. Olive realized that she wanted to lash out at her, to hurt this inquisitive old woman as much as she had been hurt herself. The cautious woman who had visited the deck in the night had disappeared, and now there was only a woman, crippled and bitter, who needed to vent her anger and despair. That was good. Truths sometimes are expelled by rage.

'Tell me about it,' she said, her tone

soothing. 'Perhaps that will make you feel somewhat better.'

'I'm not a child!' Margaret's eyes were filled with helpless rage. 'I wasn't a child even then, though I was not far from being one. You want to know what happened to me? I shall tell you, because you only think you want to know.' Her smile was a grimace of pain as the dark eyes clouded, looking inward.

'Do you recall the Algerian crisis some years ago, when the French were determined to put down the rebellion in Morocco?'

Olive nodded, her needles clicking rapidly.

'We lived there. My father's people were Bedouin, though his father had left that life and settled in the town as an accountant with the government, after being educated by missionaries. My mother was English. I was always a rebel.' Her laugh was a harsh bark, devoid of humor.

'I believed in the nationalist movement. I hated the French, with good reason. They were arrogant, incredibly callous, feeling so superior to my mother because she married my father.'

She stirred, pulling the cushions about. 'I became a courier for rebel groups in Rabat. I was fifteen, too young to know what I was risking. Too idealistic to understand that some — not all, but some — of the people I hero-worshipped were self-seeking villains who were no better than the French. They used me gladly, for I could go anywhere without rousing suspicion. I had the run of the town all my life.'

Olive's hands went still in her lap. She was afraid she knew what was coming, and she didn't really want to hear it. Tales had come out of Morocco that sickened and infuriated her.

'The French caught me with a message on my person. Do you know what the French did to women who worked with the rebels? Particularly young women? I was pretty, then too.' Her pale skin was even paler than usual,

Olive held her breath, willing the girl to go on talking. 'You see me now? Crippled? Always in pain? You should have seen me when they got through with me. Only the fact that my father was with the government took me out of their hands alive. Alive!' Her laugh sounded like a curse.

'My father sent us to England, my mother and me. It was necessary. The surgeries could not be performed in Rabat. I would not have died, of course, but the pain would have been uncontrollable. The French knew how to destroy you without killing you, I found.' She looked directly into Olive's eyes.

'And if my body should heal, miraculously, at this moment, I would still be crippled for life. Crippled on a level that will never heal, for I will die cursing those evil men on both sides of that war. I will die cursing my surgeons because they did not arrange for me to die.' She looked away, leaving Olive to catch her breath, feeling drained and weak.

'It is a terrible story,' Olive said. 'A horrible ordeal for anyone, and particularly for a child.'

'It has eaten away at me for almost twenty years. I am old, old, though I should still be fairly young, according to the calendar.'

Olive sighed and laid her hands on top of her knitting. 'Bitterness will not kill you, but it will make your life miserable. Worse than pain. Let it go, my dear. Let it go and find something to set your teeth into. Something constructive. Hatred destroys the hater.'

Margaret shrugged. 'One can be bitter and still find useful work in the world. I think I have done that. Work that will be noted, before I die. I am tired now. Please go — Glenda is coming.'

Olive stuffed her work back into the knitting bag and rose. 'I'll go,' she said. 'But I wish you would let me be your friend. Everyone needs a friend once in a while, even you, Margaret.'

She turned from the blaze of fury in those dark eyes. Her mind was working at full speed, and she felt she had learned something useful, though perhaps not what she had hoped for. Margaret Palfrey was an angry woman, bitter enough for anything, if she happened to be convinced it would visit retribution on a world that had hurt her so desperately. There had been a fanatical light in her eyes, and fanatics were more dangerous than even the most cold-blooded killers. Righteous wrath was a dangerous propulsive force.

This cruise was a ripe plum, begging to fall into the hands of anyone unscrupulous enough to pluck it. If such a purpose lay behind her presence here, what would Margaret's function be? Who was using her? Who was Button Blivens?

14

Time crawled past as if his watch hands were glued in place. Kim grunted sleepily as others passed on deck, but no one showed any tendency to stop and talk. Margaret passed him on whispering wheels, and he watched between slitted eyelids. She didn't even glance in his direction.

By the correct hour and minute to go to the cabin, he was about to come out of his skin. After seeming so nerveless in his active service days, this troubled him. Had he come to pieces so badly while sitting behind a desk?

The corridors were quiet, for everyone was either off the ship or sitting on deck. Not even a clatter from the stewards' pantry indicated that a living soul was below-decks, except for the cleaning crew on the deck below. Would this be a dry run? Probably. He just hadn't felt it was going to be a smooth operation.

His cabin was tidy, silent, and empty.

He checked it thoroughly, but nothing had been concealed there. He went into the bathroom and showered noisily, the cool water a relief after the biting sun. He towelled and put on clean shorts and T-shirt.

Should he wait longer? Should he return to the deck? Or should he seek out the steward?

'Might as well make a clean sweep, while I'm at it,' he muttered. He opened his door and looked up and down the corridor, which was brightly lit and totally empty. All the doors were closed. Except for the usual noises of a vessel at sea, it was silent.

Dawes moved quietly along the corridor to the service pantry. He tapped a knuckle lightly against the door — and it swung open on oiled hinges.

'Steward? he called. 'I need you to . . . ' He never finished his lie.

Someone came out of the room in a rush. A fold of dark cloth enveloped Dawes, and he felt a terrible blow against his temple. Even as he blacked out, he felt himself falling.

* * *

There was a long hiatus in Kim's memory. When at last he opened his eyes, he could see nothing. It took some time to recall the cloth, the rush, the blow. It required even longer to unwind from the stuff and sit up. That hurt a lot. His head throbbed, and when he closed his eyes he saw black and purple flashes.

At last he pulled himself upright, holding onto the door frame. Again blackness whirled behind his eyes, but he steadied himself and held on hard to the wood. When the dizziness eased a bit, he risked a glance into the pantry.

He knew what he would see, as soon as he sorted out what had happened to him. He just hadn't known how the murder would have been done.

It was ugly. A small man in uniform was skewered to the wall with ice picks through his palms. He sagged from his hands, head drooped forward, knees bent. Trickles of blood had run down his arms and were drying, already more brown than red.

He had seen worse, but that had been in the midst of situations he expected to be both dirty and dangerous. This was nastier because of its unexpectedness.

He forced himself to enter, to examine the man and the room. There were glasses, a cabinet of liquor, which probably had not been touched on this health oriented voyage. Linens, neat stacks of towels, vases . . . nothing was there that shouldn't be.

He lifted the man's head and looked into his face — and gagged. He had been worked over by an expert. The face looked like hamburger, the nose flattened to one side, the eyes bruised lumps, the mouth a ruined gash. The hair had been dark. What he had looked like alive Dawes couldn't guess.

All the pockets of the uniform were ripped out. Nothing could possibly have been overlooked, yet Dawes had a feeling the man had left some clue to his murderers. He had been brave; nobody who wasn't would have dared what he had dared or, obviously, suffered what he had without speaking. Such a man would not let those who misused him get away with it, if there was anything at all he could do about it.

Dawes looked around again, forgetting the throb in his head, the weakness in his knees, and the hellish pain in his leg. He knelt on the floor, wincing as he went down, and put his cheek down flat to sweep his gaze over the area under the service table, the rolling cart, the bottom-most of the shelves.

Something glinted beneath the shelves. Something small and round and silvery.

Dawes fished it out and looked closely. It seemed faintly familiar — he had seen something like it recently, though he couldn't recall just where or when. Very recently — on Margaret Palfrey's wheel-chair?

Dawes hauled himself upright and used his handkerchief to keep from leaving prints on the serving cart he used as a hand-hold. He saluted the limp shape on the wall and backed out of the pantry.

The pile of dark cloth was still in a heap on the floor, looking like something that might be used as a dust cover. He folded it carefully and tucked it beneath his arm. If it didn't belong in the pantry, it wasn't going to be found there.

The clean-up crew was still working on the deck below. He had noticed it when he was on deck. He found a rolling cart loaded with soiled linens, and buried the cloth deep in the load. Then he went back on deck, after checking in a mirror to see there was no outward trace of the blow on his head. There was no sign, though the way he felt his entire skull should have been one vast bruise.

It was a relief to sink into the deck chair and let his aching head rest. Someone had unearthed his contact, obviously, but had they also caught on to his role in the matter? Was the Stokes identity now more of a hazard than a help? He had to inform Axe at once, using the code they had arranged for communication, if the task had to be aborted.

He took the silvery knob from his shorts pocket and looked at it again. A threaded hole that would fit onto something about an eighth of an inch in diameter — it was a finishing piece, and if it wasn't off Margaret's chair he didn't know where else it might have come from.

Had the steward, perhaps lying on the floor at the time, managed to unscrew it and roll it under the shelving without his attackers noticing? No one would ever know.

Or was this something entirely different? His head whirled and throbbed. He might be doing Margaret a terrible injustice, he thought, feeling dizzy and disoriented. He put the thing back into his pocket and drifted into a troubled and feverish sleep.

'My lord! I thought he was just being lazy,' were the words that woke him. He looked up to see Olive staring down at him, her hands on her plump hips. 'He's really sick. Call the doctor!'

'No!' His voice came out a croak. 'No, don't. The doctor would find that . . . I've been cracked on the head. I can't be connected with . . . anything.'

Scarlatt, looming over his shorter companion, stared down at him, then at Olive. As if he had spoken, she nodded and turned away to walk along the deck, leaving them alone in their secluded corner.

'I have known all the while that you are not Stephen Stokes,' the Colonel said. 'I have been in this business for much longer than you, young man, and I know everyone who has ever been an operative, either in Great Britain or the United States.

'You are Joachim Dawes, of the Agency. Your code name is — or was — Drillbit, and you retired from active duty four years ago after being badly injured in an abortive operation. As far as I know, you have been on desk duty since that time.

'Now, what is the problem?'

With a sense of overwhelming relief, Kim told him the story. Axe was more than an ocean distant. This rock of a man was at hand, dependable, and at least as knowledgeable as Axe. Perhaps even more so.

He hardly raised an eyebrow as the tale unfolded.

15

When Kim finished his story, Scarlatt sat silent for a moment, as if digesting the information carefully. Then he sighed. 'The disposition of the body was a deliberate warning to someone. The killers intended for him to be found by the next person to visit that pantry, which would occur as soon as the passengers began arriving back on board.

'We must thwart them. I cannot say precisely why this is, but every instinct I possess tells me so.'

Kim stared at Benjamin, startled. 'With the ship full of people? It's impossible.'

Scarlatt shook his head. 'Olive and I came back early. Got tired, hired a boat, and returned instead of going inland with the others. Except for the crew and cleanup people, we may be the only ambulatory passengers aboard.'

Scarlatt's face was flushed with interest. 'It will be entirely feasible to remove the poor fellow from his present position, perhaps even to get the body overboard.'

Dawes sat upright but had to lean back and hold his head in both hands to still its reeling. 'In my profession, we do illegal things often. I don't want to get you into hot water,' he muttered. 'You can't afford to get mixed up in this.'

Scarlatt turned a dangerous shade of crimson, as he laughed silently. 'I have done things that would shock even you, I suspect. My career is a long one, spanning a very messy war and any number of nasty skirmishes. We have no time to waste arguing, my boy. We must get Olive and go at once to clean up the mess before the assassin's aims are achieved.'

'Olive?' Kim asked. 'Surely you don't want to get her into this.'

'My dear boy, don't be naive. I have been judging characters for twice your lifetime almost, and I can assure you that the lady will accept the situation calmly and will deal with it efficiently. There is more to Olive Rienzi, I am fully persuaded, than either of us might think.'

Scarlatt reached down and hauled Dawes to his feet, though it took a moment before he could stand without wavering. Then he steadied, and the two went after Olive, who was just returning from her circuit of the deck.

'We're going to my cabin to play a game of gin,' said the colonel, as they came up with her. 'Do you want in? The sun is getting to be too much for Stephen, I think.'

She smiled. 'It's just about too much for me too. I'd love to come.'

They passed a steward coming from the direction in which they were going. They passed one of the physical therapists, who was taking advantage of the absence of her charges to lie on deck and get a tan. Even in his present condition, Dawes felt his gaze drawn to the long expanses of honey-colored skin, but Olive tugged at his elbow.

'Come on, Stephen. You're looking a bit pale.'

They attracted no attention as they made their way to Benjamin's cabin, which was situated near Olive's and down one corridor and up another from Dawes's.

As soon as no one was within earshot, Dawes said, 'I'd better take you to . . . him . . . now. I don't know how long this bump on the head is going to affect me . . . I keep going in and out of focus.'

'You go with Olive,' Scarlatt said. 'She'll deal with that end. I shall go and commandeer a cleaning cart. I saw the area where they are stored on one of my excursions when I couldn't sleep. You go ahead together.'

He headed purposefully in one direction while Olive and Dawes took the opposite. In a few moments they were approaching the pantry, and Kim was relieved to see that he had pushed the door shut before staggering away from the scene of the murder.

Olive whisked them inside before he knew she had moved. He watched in amazement as the grandmotherly looking little person examined the corpse, even the ruined face, with the detachment of a surgeon.

Olive nodded with satisfaction when

she determined that most of the blood had soaked into the man's own clothing, leaving only minor blots and smears on the floor and the bulkhead to which he was pinned. 'That will come off without a trace. I'll take him down when Benjamin gets here with the cart. There's no use in getting blood spread about any more than it is.' She glanced at him sharply.

'Stephen, you sit down on that stool. You look as if you're about to drop.'

He obeyed, though his head was beginning to steady. He now felt nauseated, however, and he had known enough blows to the head to understand what was happening. He needed to lie down for a long time.

Olive took a towel from a stack and dampened it in the sink. The blood came up, leaving no trace. She rinsed the towel clean in clear water and wiped the sink until it was dry and shining.

'This will go into Benjamin's cleaning cart. He should have found one by now, I should think.'

Even as she spoke, there came a tap at the door. She opened it a crack, and

Scarlatt's voice said, 'Let's get him aboard quickly.'

The cart would not fit into the pantry, but in seconds the two had unpinned the victim, folded with towels to stop any late drop of blood, and laid him in the deep cart. An array of dirty linens covered him tidily. Then Olive made a last check of the pantry.

With painstaking thoroughness, she wiped down the plane surfaces and polished all the others. When she was done, Dawes felt certain that no finger-print remained anywhere, even on the undersides of shelves.

Scarlatt had found a white jacket and cap somewhere on his search, and clad in them he looked every inch a cleanup man. He trundled away down the corridor toward his own cabin, which had already been cleaned for the day. Dawes followed Olive obediently to his own, where he found himself tucked into bed with speed and efficiency.

'You stay put,' Olive ordered him. 'Rest all day. If you're not up to activities tonight, Benjamin and I will attend to getting rid of the body ourselves. I'll send you some orange juice. You don't want to eat heavily for a while. Now sleep, Stephen. I'll look in on you from time to time.'

'Yes, mother,' he said in an amused tone. He grinned up at her, though even his face was sore. 'I didn't really believe Scarlatt when he said you could deal with this sort of mess. Who are you, Olive? Really?'

Her face went still, and her eyes assessed him closely. She gave the ghost of a nod. 'One day, when there is time and when I have finally decided to retire from my calling, I shall tell you exactly who I am. Until then, you get some rest.'

'I'll tell you about me,' he said, aghast at what he was doing. 'I work for the Agency. My name is Dawes.'

She nodded. 'Good. Now I know. We'll talk about it later. Sleep.'

As soon as the door closed behind her, he closed his eyes and darkness flooded over him.

16

Olive was as good as her word. She kept glancing into Stephen's room all afternoon, and she didn't hint, when the weary tourists came aboard again, that he might be ill. She didn't want the doctor poking about and finding the lump on his skull.

All the while, her mind was busy with this unexpected discovery. She hadn't a clue as to whether it might in some way impinge upon the project she had been sent here to accomplish, though it seemed unlikely. Yet she had learned long ago not to believe too strongly in coincidence.

Upon reflection, she found she had already decided to dump any connection with those who hired her to abduct Benjamin Scarlatt. He was someone she liked and respected, and she had no intention of allowing him to be used as a pawn in the sort of power play that might have motivated her employers. Genno had not informed her who those might be, but she had dealt too long with shady characters not to catch the distinctive odour of organized crime.

She felt certain that dealing with the steward's body would fall to her and Benjamin. Dawes didn't look as if he'd be up to much for some time; head injuries were tricky anyway. It was better to be safe than sorry.

She wondered now if she should tell Scarlatt about the plot forming around him. It wasn't fair to let him go ahead blindly, when she knew his abduction was supposed to take place very soon now. Besides, they were fellow conspirators, and it was necessary that he know what he might be facing.

The *Victorine* was not a party-boat. The ill and elderly who travelled on her were not game for late movies or dances, and the ship was usually silent by ten-thirty. This night was even earlier, for everyone was exhausted from the long day of sight-seeing.

At midnight, Olive slipped from her cabin and scratched gently on Benjamin's door. He, too, was dressed in dark pants and pullover, with a dark blue cap hiding his white curls.

She chuckled. 'We look like two black dumplings.'

He took the handles of the cart and moved it to the door. 'Let us hope we are invisible black dumplings,' he said, as she opened the door and stepped aside.

The corridor had been dimmed for the night. No one stirred as they passed the doors, behind which they could hear occasional and very varied snorts and snores, as well as one spasm of coughing.

At one point, footsteps came along a cross corridor, and they scurried around a corner and held their breaths until they passed. Then they almost ran, the cart moving silently on rubber wheels, to the big service elevator that moved between the hold and the uppermost decks. Once inside it, they felt temporarily safe.

The lowest deck was crew's quarters, so they avoided that. Next up was the one set aside for the least active passengers. There they stopped and checked the corridor before bringing out their cartful of corpse.

No sooner were they clear of the elevator than a door opened down the corridor. A nurse backed out, talking to someone behind her and holding a medical tray.

' . . . Yes, doctor. I'll get it at once.' She turned and they scooted the cart back into the elevator and moved it up one deck. There they waited for a few moments, holding the elevator at that level.

When they went down again, the way was clear. They slid across the corridor and into a side passage. Beyond the glass doors the deck was dark. No passenger on this deck should be physically able to take a midnight stroll.

The nameless steward went over the side silently, dropping into the rush of water behind the fantail. The cart went with him, bobbing along for a moment, a blob of paleness against the dark waves.

There in the darkness, Olive and Benjamin stripped off their dark sweaters. Olive's turned inside-out and became pale blue. Benjamin carried his over his arm, revealing a yellow knit shirt. They linked arms and strolled along the deck to a companionway, which they climbed

146

to their own level. Both were fairly well winded by the time they arrived.

Olive turned to Scarlatt and said, 'I have something to tell you — something you have to know. It may not have a thing to do with this, but you need to know, anyway.'

He grunted agreement. 'Let's check on our patient first,' he said. 'Then we can go. Not to my cabin — I still feel that poor blighter in there. To yours?'

She nodded. 'Here, I have Stephen's key. Just a minute.' She opened the door a crack and looked in. The dim light she had left burning showed him sleeping normally, looking as if he had gained a bit more colour.

'Now we can talk.' Olive led the way toward her own cabin.

There they sank into deep chairs and sighed simultaneously. Scarlatt looked at her and began to laugh. 'I just cannot become accustomed to being an old crock,' he said. 'Inside I feel as young as I ever was, but the equipment is becoming a bit run down.'

'I never would have guessed it from the

way you have been sashaying around tonight,' Olive replied. 'I have to admit I'm feeling my years myself. This is work for youngsters, I'm afraid. I took up the trade very late in life.'

'What trade?' he asked.

She studied his face for a long moment before she answered. 'I think I can trust you not to blow the whistle on me. I have no desire to spend my last years in prison.'

'Prison? What might you possibly have done to warrant that?'

'Among other things, I am an assassin. Did you ever hear of the Knit Lady?'

Scarlatt's eyes widened. 'I do keep up with matters across the Atlantic. You mean that you are . . .'

'I am the Knit Lady.'

'Taking a holiday?' he asked, looking puzzled.

'On assignment. But I do not accept assignments blindly, and I warned the people who hired me — at least my spokesperson did — that I do not work against my ethics. I have dumped the job, though they don't know that yet.'

There was a tap at the door. Olive looked at Benjamin, who let out a deep breath and nodded. She rose and opened the door.

'Mrs. Rienzi, a message came for you today. I tried several times to find you, but you weren't in your cabin, and I thought you went on the tour. I'm sorry it took so long to get it to you.' The Purser handed her an envelope to her and smiled at Benjamin. 'Having a quiet chat? This cruise is wonderful for that.'

As the door closed behind him, Benjamin snorted. 'If we were thirty years younger, he would have hinted at much more exotic things than a quiet chat. Young snip! I can still rise to more than chit-chat, on occasion.'

Olive sank into her chair, shaking with laughter. 'I am sure you can. Tonight should prove that as nothing else could.'

She tore open the end of the envelope and looked up. 'I hope you don't mind? I've been waiting for word from someone, and this must be it.'

Once deciphered, the message was short. 'The person about whom you inquired has been identified as an associate of the Al-Fattah group based in Syria and Libya. Took name of English mother. Do not be deceived by seeming disability. Very dangerous.'

The code, of course, sounded totally harmless, but she pieced out the meaning in a few minutes, using the keys she had memorized. 'Oh dear,' she sighed. 'More complications.'

Scarlatt sank back in his seat and folded his hands on his stomach. 'Tell me.'

'I was sent on this cruise by parties into whose identity I did not inquire too closely, though they were told of my requirements. My mission was to befriend you, to become a close associate, in order to sedate you, on a given signal, and assist in your abduction. That was all I was hired to do and all I agreed to do.

'Of course, at that time I did not know you. I knew your reputation, but I also understood ... how deceptive reputations can be. Sealed into my orders, once I was aboard and opened them, I found an addendum. I was to accompany you to your place of confinement and to kill you, once the object of the exercise was achieved.

'I decided at that point to abort the mission. Later I decided to make sure the abduction didn't take place at all. I liked the notion of spoking their wheels at their own expense.'

Scarlatt closed his eyes for a long moment. When he opened them, they looked steel-bright. 'And that message?'

'At this point I can't say if it may be connected with my original mission. It concerns Margaret Palfrey, who is with Al-Fattah. Dangerous. My informant doesn't say that lightly.

'I cannot believe she would be on this cruise for her health. Margaret is a bitter woman, and people like her don't do anything without a compelling purpose. She's a fanatic — she was captured by the French in Morocco.'

She knew she need not say more. His expression told her he understood what that captivity had meant.

Scarlatt took out his pipe and lighted it. When it was going well, he looked out of a cloud of aromatic smoke and said, 'You must know about our friend Dawes.'

'He told me he's with the Agency.'

'Good. I know more, however. My work lay in similar fields. His full name is Joachim, or Kim, Dawes, code name Drillbit. He was a top agent for many years, until he was badly injured some time ago. I feel certain he is no more on this trip for his health than is our friend Margaret. His task, I do not doubt, dealt with that unfortunate steward. The mission may or may not be intertwined with whatever purpose sent you here to kidnap me. It is a tangle, isn't it?'

'This seems more like a gathering of spies than a cruise for disabled millionaires,' Olive said. 'Here I am, Margaret is, Ste . . . Kim is, you are. Not to mention our late friend now cruising without a boat.

'That's too many for mere coincidence. There are more people aboard who don't seem quite right to me, as well. I get a tingle when I think about them.

'What on earth is going on?'

17

Dawes woke slowly, feeling groggy. There was a sharp pain in the right side of his skull, and it was some time before he recalled the reason for it. Then it all came flooding back.

The bedside clock said it was nine-thirty. A sliver of sunlight struck through a gap in the curtain over his porthole. Shuddering, he pushed himself up and stood. Today, he knew, everything would hit the fan.

The steward's body would be found — or had already been found — and he would have to come forward with his story about finding it earlier. Perhaps the knock on the head would excuse his tardiness in reporting it.

He seemed to remember something else — someone had offered to get rid of the body. Scarlatt? Yes, he had said he and Olive would dispose of it and clean up the mess.

Dawes laughed, which made his head pound. What could two elderly people do?

He staggered into his shower and let alternately hot and cold water shock him to alertness. When he looked into the mirror to shave he could see little trace of the blow to his head, for the mark was covered by his mop of sandy-grey hair. One eye looked a bit puffed, but it wasn't really noticeable. He looked passable, though not at the top of his form.

Kim needed something in his stomach, which was feeling hollow. He vaguely recalled drinking juice, the night before. Olive brought it . . . yes. The empty glass was still beside the bed. But now hunger was as much a cause of his dizziness as the knock, he felt.

He moved cautiously to the dining room, greeting fellow passengers along the way. He was late, but a bland breakfast shored up his insides and eased his headache. Spirits lifting somewhat, he sought out his corner behind Olive. He might as well talk it over with her and Benjamin before going to the captain with his story. He had wondered why there was no talk of the death over breakfast, but Olive would tell him.

Then his full memory came back with a rush. The body had been removed from the pantry. He had a mental picture of the portly shape of Scarlatt trundling away with the laden cleaning cart. What had the two done with the body?

Why had he allowed them to become involved with what was, after all, an Agency matter? He must have been suffering more from concussion than he realized at the time.

Dawes found his friends talking quietly in their usual places. His own chair waited for him, and he sank into it with a sigh of relief.

Olive looked him over critically. 'You don't look too bad. Yesterday you were death warmed over, but now you only look interestingly fragile. You'll have Elizabeth all over you, wanting to comfort and cosset. Better watch out.' Her grin was pure wickedness.

Kim smiled, with some effort. 'What did you two do with . . . that?'

Scarlatt blew a curl of pipe smoke into

the breeze. 'We dealt with it. He will never come to light again, at least not in connection with the *Victorine*. On some lonely coast he may drift ashore for the puzzlement of the locals, of course.' He glanced at Dawes and turned suddenly serious.

'We had no time to give him a decent funeral. It was too rushed and too dangerous, but we kept him from being used for the purposes of those who killed him. Somehow, I believe he might have settled for that.'

The smoke drifted away on the breeze as the vessel heeled. A deck chair farther along the deck slid against the rail.

Olive looked out over the water. 'I think we may have some heavy weather. See how choppy the waves look? Not smooth and oily, the way they've been for so long. And there's a dark cloud coming up — see over there?'

Dawes looked after her pointing finger. Oh great! First a corpse, now a storm. His mission was blown, maybe his cover as well, and now this.

'We should take cover in my cabin. I

have a bottle of cognac that is strictly against all the rules, but I believe we need it. Come along with me,' Scarlatt said. He heaved himself upright and waited for the others to join him.

Even as they made their way along the deck, the vessel began to roll more abruptly, promising worse to come. Dawes had been at sea enough times to recognize the signs.

They wound up at last in Olive's cabin, after a detour to get the cognac. The liquor ran like fire through Dawes, who understood that it wasn't indicated after a head injury but who didn't care at the moment. It comforted his spirit, which was what he needed.

When they were settled into Olive's comfortable chairs, a glass at each elbow, he looked from one to the other. 'Now tell me. I can see something in your eyes. What is going on?' He sipped from his glass and sighed with pleasure. 'And what did you do with the body?'

'We told you. We put it overboard last night. No one saw, no one has said a word, though I feel certain the man has been missed by now. As for what is going on, I wish I could tell you. I don't exactly know myself.'

Olive reached for her own glass.

Looking his most dignified and judicial, Scarlatt said, 'There are too many people aboard who are involved, one way or another, with either terrorism or organized crime or with espionage.

'You are with the Agency, and I assume you were sent on a mission that involved that unfortunate steward. There is also Margaret Palfrey — yes, Margaret. She is involved with Al-Fattah, and we cannot believe she has no ulterior motive for cruising aboard the *Victorine*. I am here, though as far as I can determine there was no deliberate intention on the parts of my doctor and associates to put me in danger. And Olive is here.'

Dawes stared at her. As usual, she looked neat, grandmotherly, gentle, her fingers busy with her knitting when she wasn't sipping from her glass. He wondered if she had made up her mind to tell him the thing she'd hinted at the evening before, but Scarlatt was still speaking.

'Of course, your steward was also involved in whatever brought you here. Olive is convinced that Button Blivens is not what he seems, though she has not yet told me her reasons for that belief. Are you ready to clarify that, my dear?'

Her fingers went still for a moment, and she frowned. 'I was on deck one night when I couldn't sleep. The deckchairs had been folded out of the way, so I propped myself up under the lifeboat davit, so I wouldn't roll overboard if I fell asleep. It was one of the few really dark places on deck.' She sipped from her glass and began to knit again.

'Margaret came on deck in her chair and met with Blivens in the same patch of shadow that covered the davit. It was a business meeting of some kind — I didn't understand the language, but you cannot mistake it when people are talking turkey, particularly when they are counting.

'I do not understand Arabic, or whatever it was, but I would swear she counted to twenty, very slowly, as if to emphasize something. They talked for some time, and then they left, not together. I waited a long time before I left, as well.'

She looked at Dawes. 'What do you make of that?'

He forgot the question he had still not asked. 'It smells like terrorist activity, without a doubt. And if she is with Al-Fattah . . . it would tie up. The man I was to meet was supposed to deliver information concerning terrorist plots in Libya.

'Do you suppose . . . ' — He stared into space for a moment — ' . . . that those two killed my contact? I can see their wanting him silenced, if they knew what was happening, but why did they leave him as they did, advertising, so to speak, their action? Why want to put the ship into a panic, which would have happened if I hadn't found him and someone had discovered the way they left him?'

'More to the point,' Scarlatt rumbled, 'why didn't they come after you? Surely they saw you when they bowled you over and draped you with that cloth. Was it because they had no idea whom he was to contact aboard ship?'

'And does any of this tie into the job I was sent here to do?' asked Olive.

Dawes felt suddenly disoriented. 'What job was that?' he asked her.

'As I have just about decided to give up my career, I suppose there is no reason to keep you in the dark. I am . . . ' — she glanced sideways at Scarlatt — ' . . . the Knit Lady.'

Kim Dawes set down his glass with a thump that set the remnant of the cognac to sloshing. 'The . . . Knit . . . Lady? You?' It took a moment to absorb her words. Then he asked, 'But why are you here?'

'To abduct and later to kill Benjamin Scarlatt. I have some idea who may have hired me, though it was done through a contact. However, I can't prove it, so it is irrelevant.'

Kim found himself staring at her, tried to look away, then gave up. He had always thought the Knit Lady to be a man, one clever enough to conceal his identity in this unique way. To find that his chum of the cruise was an assassin came nearer to shocking him than anything else in almost twenty years.

Scarlatt took out his pipe and began packing it. 'It simply cannot be coincidence. Too many different elements have come together entirely too neatly. What do they all have in common, aside from taking this increasingly suspicious cruise?' He flourished the pipe stem to include them both.

'I was sent specifically to get you,' Olive said. 'We know that without any doubt. What interest or project would be greatly assisted by your being held hostage? I was told emphatically not to kill you until word came down the line that their purpose had been achieved. They didn't want you dead — that would have been easy, as we have just proven. Passengers sometimes go overboard quite innocently.

'No, they wanted you alive, in their hands, as a hostage, perhaps, able to prove yourself alive at the proper moment. Think, Benjamin. What would be achieved by something like this?'

Scarlatt set his glass beside his pipe on the table at his elbow. He folded his hands on his portly stomach and closed his eyes. When he opened them they resembled chilled steel even more strongly.

'I was fairly deeply involved in two matters. One is a military affair of which I cannot speak. I seriously doubt it could possibly apply here. The other was involved with a rumour, hardly that really, more of an intuition, that elements of an international crime syndicate were infiltrating certain portions of British business and shipping.

'I have been working quietly, correlating a number of reports, bits of data, statistics, into a comprehensive pattern. The more I got, the more it looked as if our suspicions might well be true.' He sighed heavily.

'Then a combination of age and weariness got the better of me, and I made the mistake of visiting my physician. He insisted, reinforced by my superior, that I take this cruise. So here I am.'

'When did they talk you into taking the cruise?' asked Olive.

'In May. Early in May, as I recall. Why?'

'I was approached about this assignment early in June. How did they know so quickly that you were going to do this?

163

Except for you and your doctor, who knew about your decision?'

'Even my daughter didn't know for some time,' he said. 'We certainly didn't advertise it in the Press.'

'Someone has a pipeline into your Ministry,' she said, looking grim.

'Might you be the target of terrorists?' Dawes asked, fascinated by the ideas that thronged in his head after Olive's comment.

'I shouldn't think so, though it is remotely possible. I have not been active in my old outfit for a very long while. This new generation of terrorists probably have never heard my name.'

'Anyone involved in our business knows about you,' Dawes said. 'This simply cannot be coincidental with your presence on this cruise. Either you were manipulated into coming, or someone learned you would be here and more than one plot now revolves about you.

'It would be awkward for your country to have you held as a hostage. You are a legitimate hero, you know. *The Times* would go into spasms, in a dignified manner, of course. Besides which, you probably know a great many things that Great Britain would give much to keep secret.' Dawes paused and lowered his aching head into his hands.

Olive's needles gave a decisive click. 'It all fits together,' she said. 'And I have the feeling that we will be forced to find out how, one way or another, before we are through.'

18

The *Victorine* made her lazy way down the west coast of Italy, enjoying fine weather after the earlier storm, as she plowed through the Tyrrhenian Sea. They stopped for several days to allow those who could to visit Rome. Many side trips were also available, and some of the more active passengers went overland to meet the ship at Naples.

Once through the Strait of Messina, they nosed up into the Adriatic, keeping their distance from Croatian waters and moving toward Venice. They paused for excursions whenever enough passengers requested that, leaving the rest to their own devices.

Olive went on enough of the excursions to keep her cover intact, but she was usually uneasy when she was far away from her charge. She had a feeling that only her efforts stood between Scarlatt and some uncomfortable (or worse) fate. Pesaro, Rimini, Ravenna, and Ferrara occupied only a part of her attention, which was focused on other matters.

However, Venice charmed her. She made Dawes and Scarlatt accompany her on a gondola trip. The three wandered through the old city, admiring and exclaiming, but all the while they kept discreet watch upon those about them.

No mishap occurred, perhaps due to their watchfulness, perhaps because none was planned.

When the *Victorine* turned back southeastward, she picked up speed. The wonders of Greece awaited her passengers. Those who boarded the ship arrived at night when the *Victorine* was well off Brindisi, anchored for minor repairs to her engines. Olive heard a bump that was not a part of the normal ship-sounds she had come to recognize, rose, and donned dark pants and sweater.

Something inside her told her this was it and urged her to haste. This was no simple collision with some object afloat but the thing for which she had been waiting ever since she and her companions had compared notes. All her instincts told her that worse was to come.

She peered through a crack in her door, but the corridor was its usual nighttime self. She almost stepped through, but footsteps sounded on the companionway at the end of the corridor. She nipped back inside and all but closed the door, keeping a tiny crevice through which she could look toward Benjamin's cabin.

Four men in combat fatigues clanked into view. They were armed with Uzis and smeared with camouflage grease. They looked as if they meant business, and she flinched as a fist pounded on Benjamin's door.

He had been the target all along, just as she thought. These were not representatives of the Brokers, who she had been certain were her employers, but bona fide terrorists. She knew the look and the smell of them.

The four disappeared into Scarlatt's cabin. The corridor was still, and there was no outcry, no hubbub from any part of the ship, though she listened hard. She sat for a moment in darkness, thinking hard. Then she got back into her nightgown, screwed her grey hair into tight pin-curls, and tied it in a net.

Donning a frilly bed jacket, she made certain her knitting bag was completely equipped and that her scalpel was in its sheath in her bra. All of their lives might depend upon her ability to seem a frightened, bewildered old lady.

If anyone checked on her, she was going to seem totally unsuspicious, if she could manage it. She got into bed and pulled the covers about her ears, even though the night was warm.

Then she waited.

19

SHORT WAVE TRANSMISSION INTER-CEPTED BRINDISI:

Objective attained. Subject now in custody. Ship under control. Await further orders.

Bint

CODE USED: #7, Al-Fattah

BROKEN BY OPERATIVE 2

SEND STATESIDE SOONEST

20

AXE:

EYES ONLY

Hacksaw reports seizure of cruise ship *Victorine* off Brindisi 20 July, 1300 hours. Suspect Al-Fattah. Monitoring shortwave transmissions. Italian authorities not yet aware of situation. All quiet aboard, as observed from covert survey vessel *Monarch*.
    Urgently request instructions.
    Screwdriver

Donald Axminster frowned at the note as if he might change its content by dint of sheer disapproval. He had been tempted to pull Dawes off the ship as soon as word came that his contact had been killed. Yet the man had earned some time in the sun, and he had thought it best to let him complete his rest cure.

It never paid to be soft. Axe had thought that cruise would do Drillbit a world of good. He'd let sentiment get in the way of good judgment, and just look what it caused. Whoever killed Namir must have had more than one reason for that act.

He reached into a drawer and took out a black telephone. Reluctantly, he touched buttons, but before he came to the last there was a tap at the door. He replaced the telephone and touched the disc that unlocked his office door.

Maude stood there, looking uncomfortable. 'Another message from Screwdriver. Here.' She thrust it at him and fled.

Again he read:

Victorine moving away from land, bearing south-southwest. *Monarch* weighing anchor and will keep surveillance via radar. Passenger list now in hand. Wealthy invalids now in terrorist hands. Request instructions.

Screwdriver

Axe sighed heavily and laid the second message atop the first. This time he completed his call:

'Mr. President? This is Axe. We have a problem.'

When the terse conversation was finished, Axe felt he'd been through a wringer. Yet he was grateful that there was a man in charge who was unafraid of quick and direct action. In an hour, many forces would be in motion.

A mini-sub would track *Victorine* to her destination. A special strike force would soon be flying toward the Med. The Navy was being alerted. If it looked dangerous for the unfortunate passengers, something would be done at once. In the meanwhile, there was nothing for Axe to do except worry.

He touched the button that summoned Maude. When she came she carried a tray of bread and butter and a pot of tea. This was a tremendous concession for her, and he appreciated it.

'Sit down,' he told her, 'and help me worry.'

She poured tea, though she slopped it into the saucers. Stirring her own, she said, 'Dawes is in a tight spot, Sir, but he is a very good man. He'll think of something useful. And remember that Scarlatt is there also. Dawes mentioned him in one report. Scarlatt helped him dispose of the dead steward. That, too, is a man to be reckoned with.'

'I wonder if the ship would have had a problem if Scarlatt had not been aboard,' Axe said.

Maude set down her cup with a clink. 'I have found a strange rumour,' she said. 'Our man in the Brokerage reports he heard the name of the Knit Lady mentioned in connection with the cruise.'

Axe's head came up, his eyes bright with interest. 'The Knit Lady? Interesting. I wonder what he was sent to do. The Brokers — hmmm. Get me everything current on their activities, here and in Europe. Maybe I can piece together some sense from this puzzle.'

It was the sort of assignment Maude loved. She returned after an hour with a huge bundle of printouts.

'Here you are. I think you will find this more than interesting. Perhaps it isn't very illuminating, but it does seem to cast a bit of light into the murk.'

He read long past his usual bedtime. When he set aside the stack of paper and turned out his light, Axe found himself in total agreement.

21

Benjamin had been dreaming about the river meadow where he had spent some of his happiest boyhood hours. The sun was shining, meadowsweet blooming. His sister Barbara was pursuing her toy boat, as it dashed recklessly down a runnel toward the river itself.

A sudden pounding on his door burst the fragile bubble of his dream. Scarlatt groaned and sat up, groping for his robe. What now?

No sooner had he unlocked the door than it burst open and someone entered his cabin, pushing him heavily onto his bed. Four men, dim shapes against the faint light from the corridor, loomed in the scanty confines of the cabin. He knew without looking closely just who and what they must be.

Olive had been correct. Those who had sent her after him were not the only people hoping to use him for their own ends.

'Dress yourself, old man! You are our prisoner, for now.' The young man's voice was harsh and heavily accented.

Benjamin did as he was told, moving even more heavily and awkwardly than his age and stiffness required. The young often thought of the old as helpless idiots. That was good, and it was best to keep them persuaded of that.

'Now lie down on the bed. We tie you very good.'

Oh damn! He hated being tied, perhaps because he had spent too much of his active career in such a position, if not tied with rope, at least bound with red tape. He lay on his belly and felt hands securing his wrists and ankles.

He knew ways to hold his muscles that would allow the bonds to loosen later, but the ropes were pulled so tightly that trickery didn't help much. He would not lose circulation, perhaps, but that was about all. The youngster who did the work knew her business.

He turned his face aside, breathing with controlled rhythm. Those in the room said nothing, but they sat against the walls, waiting patiently for something he felt he might be able to guess. Orders were on their way, it was plain.

He wondered about Olive. Had the ship been alerted to its danger? Was she safe?

And what about Dawes? Would these terrorists suspect his Agency connection? If they had known about the aborted contact with the steward, they well might.

He had nothing to do except worry, and he put in a full several hours doing just that. Light seeped between the curtains at the porthole at last, and with dawn the *Victorine* raised her anchor and began to move, building up to more speed than she had shown before. He could tell by the feel of the ship that the engines were running at full power.

There came a tap at the door. Three more, followed it. He heard one of his captors move to open it.

He had learned many Arabic dialects, and now he was thankful for that. These youngsters took it for granted that they could speak freely within earshot of this old fool.

'We shall take charge of the vessel when the passengers gather for breakfast. Those of the crew who are our people, as well as those we sent as passengers, are alert and ready. *Inshallah!*'

'*Inshallah!*'

The door closed, and Scarlatt knew he was facing a very long wait.

22

Dawes had known that something was going down. Old instinct, more than anything else, told him that. There was a real chance Margaret and Blivens had connected him with their victim. He must find a hiding place before things got nailed down too tightly.

He was in the corridor when booted feet thudded down the cross-passage. He flattened himself against the wall, but they did not turn in his direction, seeming to be headed toward Scarlatt's area. That didn't surprise him.

Dawes scurried to the service elevator. There was no sound to be heard, and he took it all the way to the lower hold. There, if anyplace, he could hide among the bales and boxes of supplies for the cruise.

He wondered what Olive would do when she found he was absent. He wondered if any of these invaders knew who Olive was, and he hoped they didn't. She was an ace in the hole, if she remained free to move about.

It was quiet in the hold, except for the throb of idling engines and the clink-clank of some kind of equipment swinging or swaying with the roll of the ship. Early in the voyage he had explored the entire vessel, more as a matter of habit than from any idea it might be vital to his survival. Now he blessed that instinct, for the storage area adjacent to the galleys would be perfect for his needs.

Now the galleys were empty, though it would not be long before cooks and their helpers would come yawning down to begin preparations for breakfast. He took the opportunity to appropriate a loaf of French bread, a whole salami, a bag of onions, a cheese, and a jar of piccalilli. He would eat, if nothing else.

He chose a spot at the back of the space allotted to bulky crates of supplies. Hundred-pound bags of flour were stacked beside others of sugar, rice, and beans. Walls of canned goods cases made a maze of the place. It would be weeks before the cooks could possibly work their way back as far as his lair.

There was a cul-de-sac at the end of one aisle of edibles, and that he barricaded with a false wall of cases. He could climb out over the top, at need, but he felt sure nobody would ever think of climbing up to peer over the top.

He made another trip to the galleys and commandeered a five-gallon pickle jar, which he filled with water. It was a job to get that into his burrow, but he managed it at last. Now, if driven to it, he could hole up for a very long time.

When Dawes was certain he had a secure line of retreat, he made his way upward again, taking great pains to remain unseen. It was still very early, and none of the elderly passengers stirred behind their closed doors. Crew members were beginning to move about on deck, preparing for the day's activities. Evidently the boarders had not yet made their presence known.

He moved to his own deck, down the corridor to Olive's door. There he tapped lightly. There was a moment of silence.

Then, 'Who is it?' quavered a frail and uncertain voice. It sounded totally unlike Olive.

'Dawes. Hurry.'

The door whisked open and he was pulled inside. 'Did you hear them?' she asked. 'Did you see them?'

He stared at her in disbelief. She looked the very image of doddering and incompetent old age.

Olive chuckled. 'One of my disguises. Works, too. Now answer my question.'

'I heard them. I didn't see them, though I barely missed getting caught. Did you see anyone? Who are they, as if I didn't know?'

'Commando types in combat fatigues, armed with Uzis. They went for Benjamin, first of all. I made sure of that before I got myself up in this rig. Terrorists, or I'm a duck.'

'You've had no problem, so far?'

'There hasn't been any sort of alarm. I suspect they'll spring the news on the crew as they come on duty. Probably they'll take charge of passengers when we get out on deck. That's the way I'd do it.'

Dawes grunted. 'So now we know. Okay, I've made myself a hideout down near the galleys. Do you know how to get to that part of the ship?'

She smiled. 'I always map out everything before I begin an operation. I know.'

'There's a corridor that runs in a grid, around the galleys, then off in four directions through storerooms. If you come off the companionway and take the first to your right, follow it to the first intersection with a cross-passage, take a left, then count three doors; you'll find yourself in a storage area full of cases of food. It backs right up to the corridor that goes around the galleys. Got that?'

She nodded. 'Down, right, left, three doors.'

'Once you're inside, it's like a maze. Keep track, now. First aisle to your left. Second right. Second right. First left. Second right. First left. Second right.

'You'll think you're in a dead end, but if you've gone correctly that end wall is cases of canned prune juice. Tuck your toes in the crannies and go up and over. Behind is my hidey-hole. If you need to take cover, it's as good a place as any and better than most. I have food and fresh water there, as well as all the stuff around it.'

'I'll remember,' she said. She looked up at him, head cocked. 'You'd better vamoose back to your cranny. They're going to be checking pretty closely, before long, on everybody they've caught in their trap. You don't want to be one of them, if they've tied you in with that poor steward. Your goose would be cooked almost before it got croaked, if you take my meaning.'

He grinned down at the ridiculous figure in the lacy bed-jacket. 'Too bad we're in such a rush. That is one sexty outfit.'

'Oh, you!' She gave him a pinch on the arm. 'Now get, while you can. I'm going to make sure Benjamin makes it out of this with a whole skin, and to do that I have to be with him, or at least near him. As far as I know, nobody suspects I'm anything other than what I seem. There's not much way you can disguise yourself as a lady of my years, so they aren't going to bother me much. Nobody ever notices old ladies who knit.'

He opened the door a crack. Nobody was in sight, and he darted down the corridor and into the idle elevator. From his stop on the lowest deck he crept into the service areas, where laundry was done. He recalled a ventilator shaft — and there it was. Big enough? Just. He nodded and made a quick trip to his stash of food to stock up for a long wait.

23

Olive felt the change as dawn arrived, though she didn't open her curtain to see. There was an indefinable feel of wind shifting, and the motion of the vessel, as it rode the gentle waves, changed as well. She heard movement on deck, as the crew went about their early morning duties.

She listened hard for harsher footsteps that had sounded the night before, but she heard nothing out of the ordinary. If Dawes had not visited her in the night, she might have begun to think she had dreamed that midnight intrusion. Probably any others who heard any unusual sound would do the same.

The light grew stronger beyond the sturdy material of the curtain. She could hear muted sounds from the cabins on either side of hers, so she rose and made herself look as old and fragile as possible. If she was to save Benjamin Scarlatt, she had to deceive a lot of people completely.

It took forever for the clock hands to mark the hour for breakfast. Although there was no hard and fast time set for that meal, on this cruise it was served cafeteria-style, and you wandered in when you felt like it. Between the hours of seven and ten, you could suit yourself.

She tied her hair, curled into a white fluff, into a coy pink silk scarf, put on a light shirt of pale blue chambray and a pleated navy skirt. Hose and pumps with low heels completed her outfit, making her look as much as possible like the flirtatious octogenarians as she could manage.

In her bra rode her trusty scalpel. In her knitting bag were the sharp steel needles, and in the middles of a couple of balls of yarn were concealed small pinches of plastique.

When she closed her own door behind her she turned toward Benjamin's cabin. It would be logical for her to check on him.

'Benjamin? Are you ready for breakfast?'

There was a moment of stillness inside,

holding, she felt with some sixth sense, both alarm and threat. Then Scarlatt's voice, deep and undisturbed, said, 'Not just now, my dear. I shall be up later, probably. I am . . . writing a letter to my daughter.'

She laughed, a brainless trill. 'I'll look for you later, then.'

Her heels tapped away up the corridor, but her mind was racing. Those four were still inside, she was certain, guarding their prisoner. Eventually, they would be relieved, but she had no idea when. Neither had she any idea how many terrorists there might be aboard the *Victorine*.

She knew there would be some among the crew, but it had sounded as if a good many more came aboard in the night. Still, it was hard to guess with any confidence. She needed to know.

Others were now leaving their cabins. Four accompanied her to the main dining room. Margaret Palfrey was already there. Glenda was not with her.

Since Marseilles, the groupings at the tables had shifted. Now Olive usually shared her table with Margaret, Benjamin, Dawes, and a couple who spoke nothing but French, which did not keep the over-aged lady from flirting outrageously with both Dawes and Scarlatt.

This morning only Margaret was there. Olive fluttered into place, not overdoing it but beginning her transition to elderly incompetent. She smiled at the younger woman. 'We're the only early-birds, I see. Benjamin was writing letters, but he said he would be on deck later. I do hope he isn't taking a cold. He sounded rather hoarse.'

Without seeming to, Olive watched Margaret intently. She was pale, her olive skin almost greenish. A nerve at the corner of her eye twitched, and her hands were clasped hard on the arms of her wheelchair.

Olive settled her knitting bag and rose to go through the food line. 'May I bring you something? As Glenda isn't here, I would be happy to.'

Margaret managed a stiff smile. 'If you would . . . just some toast and orange juice. I am . . . not hungry this morning.'

190

When Olive returned with a tray holding both breakfasts, the Montesquieus had arrived. Yvette was looking around with an air of disappointment, for no man other than her husband was within her range of activity.

The waitress came into view, coffeepot in hand. She looked shaken and kept glancing back into the serving area from which she had emerged. When she filled Olive's cup, her hand shook. That told the Knit Lady the newcomers must now have taken control of the ship.

She gazed out through the glass doors and over the sea. The angle of the sun on waves told her they were heading toward the southwest, not toward Greece, their next destination. She sighed gently and smiled up at the waitress.

'Thank you, my dear,' she said. The girl's eyes filled with tears, and she turned sharply to fill cups at another table.

It was a long wait, while stragglers breakfasted and came to congregate on the decks. Olive sat in her usual deck chair, knitting furiously. The ball of yarn she was using held explosive at its core.

She glanced up from time to time, as if looking for her two usual companions, but they did not come. At about ten-thirty, people were beginning to move restlessly from group to group, talking aimlessly. Something was wrong, and they could feel it, although nothing overt had happened.

Olive noted that no male crew member had been visible all morning. The young women who helped the cruise director seemed nervous and absent-minded, and that was communicating itself to their charges.

Even as she thought about that, Button Blivens emerged onto the deck and looked about, his pearly teeth shining in the sunlight. 'Ladies and gentlemen,' he began.

Olive tensed but made herself relax. This was it. She looked from the corner of her eye into the shadows beyond the companionway. They were there, waiting for the moment to come when they would emerge into the glare of the sun and frighten these poor old people out of their wits.

She gritted her teeth and knitted on. 'Just like Madame DeFarge,' she growled deep in her throat.

Blivens was talking now, his voice smooth as a salesman's. 'It is my duty to report that this ship has been seized by Al-Fattah, the Party for the Liberation of the Oppressed. Any resistance will be fatal, so I urge you to sit quietly and wait for further orders.'

Margaret's chair was a few yards from Olive's. The woman was sitting stiffly, her hands beneath the light scarf she kept over her knees. Nobody was watching her, every gaze being fixed upon Blivens.

Olive slipped silently forward one chair, then another. Now she was just behind Margaret. She took one needle out of her scarlet muffler and thrust it neatly into the base of the crippled woman's skull. Her other hand darted beneath the scarf and emerged holding the Uzi concealed there, beneath Margaret's pleated skirt.

Olive glanced about. Those in the companionway were still waiting, blinded by the glare on deck. The row of chairs had also screened her from view. Margaret's head was tilted against the back of her chair as if she were resting.

Olive moved back, one chair at a time, to her own place. There she wiped the small stain from her needle onto the scarlet muffler and ran the needle back into the knitting. Her needles began clicking again.

The Uzi was now hidden under her own pleated skirt. She blessed the economical size of that weapon, which lent itself to easy concealment.

'You will all now move to the afterdeck,' Blivens was saying. 'There you will be instructed as to your activities in future.'

She slipped the Uzi beneath a stack of deck chairs beside her own and rose obediently, clutching her knitting bag, with its fluff of red wool foaming over the edge. She had learned how to look totally helpless, and she used that skill now, to the fullest.

Two men in fatigues came into the sunlight and gestured with their weapons. Faint shrieks and exclamations rose from the assembled oldsters, but nobody resisted as they were all herded toward the rear deck. Olive was lost amid the group, as she knew she would be, for most of her companions were taller than she.

Taking advantage of that concealment, she put the remnant of the wool containing the plastique into her brassiere. It would probably come in handy.

When they stopped, she found herself between Madame Montesquieu and a woman she had seen about but had never spoken to. Both looked stunned. Olive matched her expression to theirs.

A large, very dark man came forward and looked over the captives in this group. He ran his gaze over the three women without doing more than noting the number. When he had examined the entire gathering, he took up his position beside Blivens, who was once more the centre of attention.

The dark man nodded, and the steward said, 'You are now captives. This means you will not move about the ship at will. You will be fed once a day, at a time convenient to us. You will remain in your cabins unless summoned for an interview. You will do nothing that might attract the attention of any vessel we might encounter, and you will not congregate in groups at any time, even when dining.'

He looked about, as if for emphasis. 'This is not a game. This is not America, where people do as they please. This is now a ship of war, and you will do as ordered, or you will be shot.'

Not a word was spoken when he finished. In groups of a half-dozen, the elderly people were herded away to their cabins. Olive went willingly. Now she would have the opportunity to decide how to free Benjamin from his captors.

24

Gianello sat in his big chair, staring out into the garden. He was furious, but he did not allow any expression of his true feelings to surface. His subordinates must believe him to be impervious to such human emotions.

This was a simple matter of business. He had chosen a suitable agent and arranged a neat, foolproof operation. Now everything was in shambles.

He was beginning to suspect that someone had a pipeline into his most secret deliberations. No one had known of Scarlatt's trip except those who were in his employ, which included the office nurse who worked with Scarlatt's physician. The tongues of his fellow Directors were not loose. They would never have attained their present positions if they had been.

That meant someone else — an unknown working for another unknown

197

— had access to his own house.

Gianello had used Al-Fattah for his own purposes from time to time. This act of piracy had all the earmarks of one of their operations. There had been no hint, on any grapevine at his command, of the Knit Lady, so he was certain it had been no slip of the assassin's that had revealed the Brokers' plot.

That meant there were spies within his household. He touched a button beneath his desk. It was not the butler who answered that bell.

A thin fellow in a dark suit entered the room through the French windows. 'Sir?' he asked.

'I want the staff ... dismissed. Permanently. Without any suspicious trace left. See to it.'

Corrigan nodded. Gianello knew he would not allow himself even to wonder about the reason for that order.

'Tomorrow is Sunday. They might enjoy a holiday,' he suggested. 'Hire a bus. Take them on a nice trip into the mountains. They should like that.'

Corrigan nodded again.

Gianello smiled at his retreating back. Then he touched another button and spoke to his secretary, who was in New York in the offices of his principal business of record.

'Put everyone you have to work on this ship thing. We must regain control of Scarlatt. We must make the . . . other organisation . . . understand we are not to be used or thwarted. Does Minski still have access to a minisub?'

'He does,' said Nuttall.

'Tell him to fly it to the Mediterranean immediately. Jeske will give him the coordinates. He can begin monitoring everything that happens.'

'Of course.'

'Get our best men into position. Corsica? No, Crete. I have connections there. Have a fast launch ready to move them into position, when the time comes to retake the ship. Put Jeske in charge of coordinating our forces. He's good at that. And Nuttall . . . '

'Sir?'

'Fire your office staff. Get fresh people from bottom to top. We have had a leak. I may want fresh servants here, in fact. Also, inform my associates that they may need to look closely at their own people. We want no repetition of this problem.'

'Yes, Sir. Is that all?'

'For now.'

Gianello relaxed, leaning back again, staring into the sunlit garden. All of it would be done and done effectively.

He hoped he could retrieve his position.

The chairman of the Brokers did not keep control if he was guilty of a failure.

25

Though he was most uncomfortable, Scarlatt had not complained. He understood better than most the emotional instability of terrorists. You didn't want to rattle them unnecessarily.

They had eventually turned him onto his back, with his head raised on a pile of pillows so he wouldn't rest directly on his bound hands. Even so, the circulation was almost cut off, as his hands swelled. His fingers felt like sausages, numb and fat feeling, along with his wrists. Arthritis stabbed through his joints with cruel regularity.

He was thinking so hard that he barely noted the pain. It had been proven that Olive was not the only person sent to gain control of his person. If her employers were not behind this, and it was illogical that they should be, for they thought their agent had the situation under control, still another organization was taking a hand.

That made two separate interests. Dawes's contact, the departed steward, had possessed information concerning terrorist activities, probably this group.

He swallowed and coughed. The leader of his guards rose from his hunkered position and came to look down at him. The black eyes were hard and emotionless. This was no fanatic urged to action by religious fervour. This was a professional, cold and deliberate. Scarlatt had understood that instantly.

The woman had also come to stand beside the bed. She was another of the same kind, he thought. Their two associates, very young, very nervous, were another sort entirely. Their eyes held the fires of religious feeling, and they would be the ones he might affect, if he had an opportunity.

He gazed up calmly. 'Well?' His tone was ironic. 'Are you making certain that I have not escaped? You can see that I have not.'

'You do not ask why you are confined,' the woman said. Scarlatt had never betrayed his understanding of their dialect, and he did not do so now. He looked at her inquiringly. 'Am I a hostage? I assume you know who I am and what my background has been or you would not have confined me so tightly.

'You have evidently seized this ship and its passengers. What are you demanding in return for freeing them? Or do you intend to kill us all?'

The man laughed, a short bark, and turned away. 'He is a fool,' he said in their language. 'He does not realize what our purpose actually is. That is good.'

Benjamin felt this proved what Olive had intuited. He was the focus of attention from more than one group, with more than one purpose. Now what was this batch trying to achieve?

He thought about that last note to Challoner. Now he had an inkling what Olive's employers might have wanted, for rumours of a criminal takeover of British shipping and crucial industries had been floating about for some time. If sufficient leverage were applied, his Ministry might be pressured in ways that nothing else might achieve. A chink could well appear in the armour of the dwindled Empire, allowing the Brokers to slip through.

That must have been the aim of Olive's assignment, but this other group was obviously not concerned with trade and industry. They wanted him for some other reason, and he couldn't imagine what it might be.

The answer came to him suddenly. Hakim the bomber was imprisoned in England, after an abortive escape attempt on Gibraltar. Though he had never been connected formally with Al-Fattah, every agency in the world assumed him to be its true leader.

Benjamin was thinking deeply when there was a knock at the door. Again the same sequence gained admittance as the woman opened the door and a burly man entered.

'We have control of the ship. All is calm, and we are headed for our own destination. As far as we know, there is not yet any alarm in any quarter. No signal has gone out from this ship, and we have detected no surveillance from the air or the water.

'You will be relieved in an hour, for there is little danger from these ancients. Most of the crew is composed of our own people, and those who are not are women and no danger to our cause. Do not, however, relax your vigilance.'

He stalked to the bedside and stared down at Scarlatt. 'You!' he spat. 'I suspect you do not recognize me and that you cannot recall our last meeting.'

Benjamin chuckled. 'Oh, my dear Ali, of course I recall, both you and our last meeting. I see that your memento of that occasion healed badly. You have a noticeable scar. What a pity I botched the job, for I intended to take off your head.'

The man recoiled, then controlled himself. He bent forward and spat into Benjamin's face. Then he turned and left the room.

Scarlatt grinned at his captors. 'Charming man, your leader. A pity he's mad as a hatter. Do watch him. I have known him to do great damage to his own followers, on occasion and if it suited his purpose.'

Swift as a tigress, the woman moved across the room. Her hand cracked across

Scarlatt's face. 'Silence! We will hear none of this.'

He relaxed and turned his face to wipe the spittle onto the pillowcase. He couldn't do much now except rattle their cages a bit. And wait, of course.

Hours passed. Food came on a tray, and one of his hands was loosed enough for him to eat. Then he was tied even more tightly while his guards ate.

More hours went by. It had to be late afternoon, from the quality of the light creeping around the edges of the curtain, when he heard something very faint and unobtrusive in the wall at his head. A scratching noise. No, more like slicing. Not quite like a mouse in the wall — did ships at sea have mice?

There came an almost imperceptible splitting sound. He looked hard at his guards, but they were playing some endless game with a board and pieces and seemed to hear nothing. The woman glanced up from time to time, but she seemed to sense nothing unusual.

Something snaked beneath Benjamin's pile of pillows and moved to one side nearest the wall. Something touched his neck. A finger. Tapping, three times. Three more. Three more.

It had to be a signal. From whom? Had Dawes eluded the terrorists? But how could he have got into the adjoining cabin?

The signal told him one thing clearly. Someone was free and on the move. Someone wanted him to be ready, when the time came, to help free himself.

He tried to flex his numb fingers that lay beneath his body and to move his cramped muscles as much as he could without betraying the effort. It would do little good if he were completely numb and helpless when aid came.

26

All the old people were shut into their cabins, the doors locked from the outside, which Olive had not realized was possible. She felt certain an armed guard was positioned at the cross corridor, where he could see up and down the lines of doorways.

If she was to rescue Benjamin, she was going to have to go to his cabin the hard way. There was one cabin between hers and Scarlatt's, tenanted by Miss Melliloe and her sister Agatha. They were so quiet and self-absorbed that Olive hadn't even tried to get to know them. Boring was the kindest term she could think of for the pair.

She went into her bathroom and stared at the wall separating it from that in the adjacent cabin. It was tile, probably backed by wallboard. She found her knitting bag and dug out a needle. This was going to be a lot of work, she decided.

It was. The tile came off in big squares, along with the backing board, a rather noisy operation, no matter how carefully she went about poking and prying. When she was down to the studs holding the wall panels in place, she found they were some fourteen inches apart.

She looked down at herself. Her svelte days were long behind her. Her bosom alone was too abundant to go through that space easily. She sighed. It would have to be done nevertheless.

She tapped briskly on the remaining panel, which faced into the Melliloes' bath. 'Miss Melliloe? Agatha? Are you there?' she called.

She heard a gasp. Then a timid voice asked, 'Who is there? Are you . . . inside the wall?'

'Of course not. This is Olive Rienzi, in the next cabin. I'm coming through the wall into your bath. I hope you don't mind if I make a bit of a mess.'

'Through . . . the wall? But how . . . ? I suppose so. Do be careful!'

Olive thrust one needle entirely through beside a panel and pried. In an older vessel, the wall might have been solid wood, but this was ply board, and she opened the join and pushed back the adjoining panels to clear the space between studs.

Again she sighed. She had donned jeans and cotton shirt, along with a knit cap that concealed her white hair. Sneakers and her knitting bag, now stuffed with everything she might need, completed her outfit.

She sucked in her gut, squeezed her bosom flat with both hands, and pushed herself painfully through the inadequate space. Her stomach felt scraped. Her hands pushed frantically, forcing her frontal development flat enough to make the passage.

Her knuckles were bleeding when she popped through into the adjoining bath. She sneezed explosively and wiped her eyes with a tissue from her knitting bag.

The Misses Melliloe stood at the door in attitudes of maidenly alarm, staring as if she were a Martian emerging from a spaceship. 'Mrs. Rienzi, it is you. I never would have recognized you . . . you look so odd.' Agatha gestured helplessly to indicate that her attire was completely unladylike.

'For the business at hand, this is best,' Olive assured her. 'I'm afraid I must make another hole in your other wall. I see . . . it's inside your closet. That helps, for it won't be so noticeable. I think you might be able to push the panelling back in place where I came through, once I'm done. Perhaps nobody will notice the holes. At least not until they look fairly hard.

'I must go now. Thank you, ladies, for your patience. I have work to do.' She pushed into the narrow closet and slid the pastel dresses along the rod until she could attack the wall. This should be at the head of Benjamin's bed, she recalled.

This time she was extremely cautious. Noise would be fatal at this point. She used her scalpel, working the keen blade carefully to break the seal of tape between two sections of panelling. She took care not to put too much pressure on the thin blade.

Her fingers cramped. The arthritis in her joints screamed with pain, but she persisted. When at last she rested for a moment, there came a light touch at her elbow.

'Would you like tea? We have our little electric kettle here, and we felt a cup might soothe our nerves. You have been working so hard — we think it might do you good too.'

Agatha's expression was still puzzled, but she exuded an air of good will as she gestured toward the small table where an enamelled kettle steamed amid blue willow teacups.

'We always bring our own things. It's so comforting, when you are in an alien setting.' That was Miss Melliloe, and it was the first time Olive had ever heard her deep voice.

They sat properly about the little table, sipping tea and nibbling shortbread from a tin box that Agatha brought out of the closet.

Olive felt strangely disoriented.

This morning, she had killed a young crippled woman. She was making her way through walls to rescue a friend from probable death. And here she sat with these incredibly ladylike and well-intentioned women, taking tea as if she were in a British parlour.

She drained her cup, brushed the crumbs from her shirt, and smiled at the two. 'Thank you. That gave me fresh energy, and do believe me, you may have helped to save someone's life. But I must get busy again. There isn't much time.'

'Do come again,' said Agatha, her reflexes taking charge. Olive laughed silently as she returned to the closet. She found that strange episodes seemed a part of her odd career, but this was stranger than most. Alice's Tea Party didn't cut a patch on this one.

When she had the hole sufficiently large to admit her hand, she closed her eyes and hoped fervently that she had estimated the height of the head of the bed correctly. She'd had no idea, when last she visited Benjamin's cabin, that she needed to make a note of that. But she worked her hand through with great caution.

As no bright light had shone through the hole, she felt she was at a reasonable level. Her fingers touched linen — a pillow with considerable weight resting on it. She pushed her hand forward, angling it toward the wall side of the bed.

Her elbow passed through the hole, giving her more maneuverability. She moved her fingers upward very slowly and touched warm skin. Benjamin, without a doubt, for the owner of the skin made no sound.

She tapped him nine times, in groups of three. He would know that help was on its way, if not when or how. Olive worked her arm back through the hole and put as much as possible of the panelling into place again. She hoped nobody on the other side would notice the damage to the wall. From the quality of the light in that other room she felt they had kept the curtains drawn and had not turned on any strong light.

She sighed and wiped her forehead.

The Misses Melliloe were gazing anxiously at her as she backed from the closet. 'Are you . . . all right?' asked Agatha. 'Did you do what you intended?'

'Some of it,' she replied. She moved to the bathroom and prepared to squeeze through that wall again. When she had gained her own bath, she heard the Melliloes putting the panel back into place.

Bless the British! They usually came up to taw, when things got sticky.

She removed her clothing and took a long shower. Then Olive dressed again in rough and ready gear, checked her knitting bag to make certain she had it properly equipped if something barred her from returning to her cabin, and lay down for a short rest.

Now came the dangerous part of her task.

27

MONARCH TO SCREWDRIVER: VESSEL PARALLELLING COURSE OF *VICTORINE*, ENE, PACING. TAKING NO ACTION. IS IT OURS?

TO *MONARCH*: ONLY MINI SUPPLY VESSEL, DUE SOUTH OF YOUR POSITION, IS OURS. OBSERVE STRANGE CRAFT. DO NOT APPROACH OR COMMUNICATE. IDENTIFY IF POSSIBLE.

TO SCREWDRIVER: SATELLITE SURVEIL-LANCE IDENTIFIES VESSEL AS *KYRIOS KRIS*, OUT OF CRETE. POSSIBLE SUPPLY VESSEL FOR MINISUB. WHOSE?

TO *MONARCH*: MAINTAIN DISTANCE, SILENCE. OBSERVE. MONITOR BAND 5 FOR COMM FROM JACOBS.

28

Intelligence networks around the Med were quivering with unexplained sensitivity. Something huge was going down, and few knew what it might be. Not one of those few was talking.

Screwdriver had now received his desperately needed instructions, and those gave him no comfort. He had wanted to be handed a foolproof plan that would deliver the helpless captives at once. Instead he was told to wait. To watch everything, take note of everything, but to make no move on his own.

Hacksaw was in charge of the *Monarch*, ranging just out of sight of the speeding *Victorine* and monitoring everything possible with sophisticated equipment. His information was relayed to Screwdriver via a secure channel, and coded to sound like normal commercial communication.

Those communications contained nothing that comforted the waiting agent. The vessel was hurrying toward some rendez-vous, that was obvious. Screwdriver was uneasy at the thought of those who might meet it, when it reached its goal.

He coordinated the groups arriving within twenty-four hours of the *Victorine*'s seizure. Commander Jacobs, with his minisub, was within convenient reach, off Corfu helping with the retrieval of a sunken bomber carrying sensitive equipment. He was on the spot almost at once, and his tiny sub took up the pursuit of *Victorine*, followed by its supply vessel, with which it had to link up periodically for fresh supplies.

A detachment of crack troops arrived at Naples, ostensibly en route to an exercise off the coast of Libya. In light of recent unrest in that area, no one, official or otherwise, was surprised at that.

They flew out again with the hour, and their route was changed fifteen minutes after takeoff. They joined Screwdriver at Brindisi, very quietly, via fishing craft.

The *Empress*, twin of the *Monarch*, weighed anchor almost at once, and the task force was on its way. That reassured

Screwdriver, although he must remain behind to monitor all the elements of the rescue teams.

Before dawn of the second day of *Victorine*'s travail, he sent a message to Axe:

TEAMS IN PLACE. NO CHANGE IN STATUS ABOARD SHIP VISIBLE. WAITING.

At last he felt as if he had accomplished something.

29

Dawes had reactivated many of his old skills in the past twenty-four hours. He traced out the ventilator systems on each deck and oriented them as to the shafts rising from the lower reaches of the vessel. Using those, he managed to reach strategic spots from which to count and assess the abilities of the uniformed men who had come aboard.

The crew members he knew; even though he was certain most had been in on the plot, they were not people he considered effective opponents. Button Blivens was fairly typical of their number. They had the ability to con the ship owners, possessed some superficial strength but little know-how and even less willingness to die for a cause.

Kim had known many times when his life depended upon his ability to size up people, and he thought he wasn't far out in his assessments. Margaret Palfrey was the one he really feared, and her disability put her at a sufficient disadvantage. He hoped Olive would watch her step.

There would be opportunities to knock off individual members of the terrorist group from time to time. That wouldn't be difficult, given the darkish labyrinth of the service decks. However, the passengers might suffer reprisals, if he took such action. That put him at an impasse.

It was soon evident that the cooks were no part of the plot. They worked in shifts, guarded by at least two men with weapons. From bits of conversation that came to his ears, as he eavesdropped in one of his hiding places, those men and women were more than unhappy with this turn of events.

He heard other things far more interesting. The bulkheads were thin, mere partitions dividing the storage areas from the corridor, and the corridor from the galleys. He found a spot beside a ventilating duct, through which he could hear what was said in the aft section of the galley.

'They intend to shoot some hostages, if

there is any sign of pursuit,' one young woman said, in Spanish, to her helper. 'Pray to the good God that we are not among them.'

'We are of no importance. They will kill one of those rich ones, if they decide on that course. You will see. We are useful. Those others, they are sick and helpless, and these *cabritos* hate them for their wealth.' It was a boy's voice. '*Gracias a Díos*, I was born poor and will always be so.'

Dawes wondered how long it would take the pirates to get around to such actions. He hoped Axe and the government were going about whatever they intended to do with the utmost care, for they might trigger a bloodbath. In the mean time, he had to find a way to keep watch on the main deck, where problems would most probably arise.

Using his convenient lock-picking skills, Dawes rummaged around the storerooms until he found an array of spare uniforms for cleanup and food service crew members. White jackets and duck trousers were provided in all sizes, and a set gave him a convincing air of legitimacy. Attired in spotless white, he joined a group of cleanup people, who were being herded a bit haphazardly up the corridor.

Evidently the guards, who were rather far behind their charges, had not counted carefully. The addition of one seemed not to disturb either of them.

He followed the others to the equipment storage and provided himself with a cleanup cart. With one other (the elevator would not hold two at a time) he went up to the main deck, rather astonished that the terrorists not only allowed but demanded that such services continue. But he could see that it kept people too busy to be plotting mischief.

Nobody in the work detail mentioned that he was a stranger to them. That was even more surprising, but he noted that all the others seemed preoccupied, probably concerned that they might be shot as hostages, like the girl in the galley. Whatever the cause, he was more than happy that this was true.

He broke out a mop and began swabbing the deck. It was barely daylight, and only his crew and their guards seemed to be stirring. He cleaned carefully and well, but he managed to work his way around out of sight of the nearest guard. He approached the side onto which Olive's porthole opened, and counting carefully he located what had to be her cabin. Keeping an eye out for any watcher, he tapped on the glass.

In a moment he heard a faint tap in return. The porthole was undogged and her voice asked, 'Dawes?'

'Yes. How goes it?'

'I killed Margaret — a knitting needle into the base of her skull. I don't think they knew she was murdered — there was hardly any blood, and I wiped that away. Her hair covered the tiny wound. They think she died of natural causes from the excitement. I got her Uzi, just in case, hid it, and I managed to retrieve it when I got them to let me go after my knitting bag.'

He felt a pang of real grief. That had been a beautiful and intelligent woman. It was a pity that her life had been warped by the cruelty of conscienceless forces.

Olive was speaking again. 'I have a bit

of plastique. I want you to stick a wad of it onto Benjamin's door. Can you do that? Not enough to blast the cabin, just enough to blow a fairish hole, so I can take him out through the wall during the commotion.'

'The wall? How in hell . . . ?'

'I haven't time to explain. Here's the stuff. Here's the detonator. And here's the tiny transmitter. Press the plunger when you want to send the signal. Set it off at about — let's see — look at your watch. Six fifteen. On the dot. Okay?'

He took the wrapped wad and stuck it in a pocket. 'Okay. Be careful, will you? And tell Benjamin I have my eyes open.' The porthole snicked shut, and he resumed mopping as a sleepy guard came stumbling around the deck, looking for him.

He worked his way all the way around, timing himself. He finished swabbing his section in time to begin polishing the brass door fittings, moving up the corridor where Benjamin's and Olive's cabins were located.

''And he polished up the handle of the

big front door' . . . ' he hummed, as he inserted the plastique into the brass fitting around Benjamin's door handle, inserted the pin-like antenna, and moved on to the next door.

'Six-eight, six-ten, six-twelve . . . ' He trundled the cart away and around the bend into a cross corridor. Six-fifteen.

He pressed the button on the small transmitter. There was a muffled explosion that brought the other guard running to join the first, who was staring up the way, startled and confused.

Dawes huddled with the other cleanup people, slipping back through the bunch as if trying to get away from danger. He emerged past the last and faded into the service companionway, and in fifteen minutes he was again in his hideaway. As soon as the porthole was closed and the curtain drawn, Olive sprang into action. She jerked the shower curtain back to reveal the damaged wall. The tile and backing boards came away, and she laid them against the wall before tapping on the panelling inside the Melliloe bathroom.

'Miss Melliloe? Agatha? I'm coming through. Don't be alarmed.'

Without waiting for a reply, she slid the inner panel aside, mashed her façade flat with both hands, and scrunched through the opening. Emerging from the bath, she found the Melliloes regarding her from their twin beds, round faces sleepy and faintly alarmed, like a pair of owls surprised in their nest.

'Go back to sleep,' she told them gently. 'You haven't seen or heard anything at all.'

Obediently they closed their eyes, and she shot into the closet and slipped the interior panelling aside. Then she got a grip on the panel facing into Benjamin's cabin, which she had already loosened. The luminous dial of her watch glowed faintly, hands creeping with terrible slowness toward the appointed time for the explosion.

She put her lips near the hole she had made before, from which she removed the neat plug of paneling she had used to stop it off. 'Benjamin,' she breathed, 'Be ready!'

She had no idea if he had heard, but she trusted to his instincts. After that, there was nothing to do but wait, and it felt like hours.

Even though she expected it, the explosion made her jump. Then she was slipping the loose panel out of the way.

Nobody human would be watching the captive when the door had just been blown to Kingdom Come.

Her scalpel sliced Benjamin's hands free, and he turned awkwardly to face her, standing on his knees on the bed. He forced his bulk through the gap between the uprights, and she backed ahead of him out of the closet. Once he was through, Olive shot back to pull the interior panel back into place, plug the hole, and replace the panelling on the inside wall. She stacked the Melliloes' suitcases against it to hold it in place and pulled their dresses across the rod.

When she backed out of the closet, its interior looked completely innocent. Olive didn't pause, even though the Misses Melliloe were now bundled in challis robes, twittering questions at Scarlatt.

'Go back to bed,' Olive ordered them. 'Be frightened, but don't know anything. Come, Benjamin.'

He went ahead of her, already groaning as he mashed his ample shape between yet another set of uprights. She followed him into her tiny bathroom and turned, once again, to secure the panelling, this time with tape. She hoped it would not show from the other side that it had been removed and replaced.

She hated to think of the Melliloes being shot because of her, but better them than Scarlatt.

They tried their best to restore the bathroom wall in the time they had. It didn't look bad, but you could tell something had happened to it.

'How do we get out of here?' Scarlatt whispered, staring about. 'They'll search every cabin on the ship until they find me.'

'I know that,' she said. 'You watch through the porthole from behind the curtain. When the deck is clear, let me know.' She fumbled in her knitting bag and pulled out a ball of red yarn.

'Three men are running along it. They just went out of sight. Nobody is there now,' he reported.

Olive put her ear against the door and listened intently. Many heavy feet stirred in the corridor. The terrorists had to be in a state of shock now. This was as good a time as any.

Olive stuck a ball of plastique, carefully estimated, against the bulkhead beneath the porthole. She placed the antenna neatly and motioned for Benjamin to join her in the bathroom again, which was a tight fit. She pressed the plunger of the transmitter, and the world erupted into chaos.

Scarlatt pushed aside the buckled door of the bath and bent to stare through the gaping hole in the wall. The deck was still deserted, Olive noted.

They crawled through, Olive's bad knee twinging painfully, and stood on the open deck. 'That way, to the elevators,' she said, getting a firm grip on her knitting bag with one hand and readying the Uzi with the other.

They ran as quietly as possible down

the deck, turned into the area backed by the elevators, and flattened against the wall as more footsteps pounded toward them. Two fatigue-garbed men rounded a corner and came face to face with the pair.

Olive swept them with a squirt of fire from the Uzi, and they fell into awkward attitudes, though one still squirmed and moaned. She left him to it, as she followed Scarlatt into an elevator and pushed the DOWN button.

They left the elevator at the next deck down, and she led the way to the companionway Dawes had described. The confusion above seemed not to have spread this far as yet, and nobody was moving in the corridor as they emerged into it. Going around the prescribed bends, Olive muttered right and left as she recalled the directions she had memorized. They found the storeroom and negotiated the maze, finding themselves at the dead-end wall of cases.

'Dawes?' Olive said softly. 'Are you there?'

She heard a faint stirring behind the

wall. In the dimness, a pale face appeared over the top.

'Well, well. Company. I wondered if you'd make it,' said Dawes. 'Come on up and over. It's going to be healthier for us if we stay put for a while. I suspect this ship is going to be searched from stem to stern, and I just hope we and the rats manage to stay out of sight.'

Scarlatt managed a tight chuckle. 'I seem to be the object of the entire exercise. I wonder what they intended to achieve? But we've put a spoke in their wheel now.' He turned to Olive, who was leaning against a wall of crates, trying to get her breath.

'My dear, do let me assist you. I suspect those knees may be giving you hell by now.'

She smiled. Trust Benjamin to act the gentleman, no matter what. All she said, however, was, 'Thank you,' as she accepted his boost and scrambled up and over into Dawes's hideaway.

30

TO CHAIRMAN:

UNABLE TO APPROACH VICTORINE. SUB-
MARINE CRAFT SHADOWING VESSEL
CLOSELY. SUSPECT U.S. MILITARY. AGENTS
CRETE AFFIRM AL FATTAH INVOLVE-
MENT. NEED FURTHER ORDERS.
   MINSKI

Gianello crumpled the message and
flung it toward the basket. Was there no
end to the interference he must deal
with?

Corrigan, summoned, entered by way
of the glass doors to the garden. 'Sir?' His
tone was incurious, as usual.

'Everyone involved in this operation
must be eliminated. Genno himself, if
that is possible, must go. The Knit
Lady. Minski. The entire New York
office staff.' He stared into the man's
impassive face. 'Send this message to

my Board. At once.'

Corrigan took the scribbled page from his hand, glanced at it once, and nodded. It was a relief to have one who cared nothing for success or failure, for murder or survival. Orders were all that mattered to Corrigan.

It galled Gianello to think of the content of that note. To admit failure — he had not been able to manage that, as yet but this was much to close to it:

OPERATION SCRUBBED, DUE INTER-FERENCE AL FATTAH. WILL INFORM NEW PLAN FOR BRITISH INVOLVE-MENT SOON. CHAIRMAN.

Those words still rankled. He refused to allow menials who knew of his failures to live. All, with the exception of Corrigan, would die. Genno was a remote maybe, but if he could be eliminated, that too would be done.

The new cook's efforts drew him from his thoughts, and he sat down to his meal. When he rose he was determined to replace this cook too, possibly condemning her to death as a menace to the human digestion.

Gianello placed no value on any life except his own.

31

The ship echoed to the efforts of the searchers. Even in the storeroom beyond their artificial wall of cases, bales and boxes and bags had been moved about, crashing into untidy heaps, while the angry terrorists poked and pried among them.

Lying packed like sardines in their cramped space, the three fugitives held their breaths while the frontal wall of cases underwent attack. But Dawes had shored it up strongly from the rear, building buttresses of boxes braced against the wall. There was no indication that space existed behind that barrier, and the seekers gave up at last.

The terrorists had shouted comments as they worked, and though Olive couldn't understand a word she felt Benjamin, jammed tightly against her side, tense as if he listened closely. When the last left the storeroom and the door slammed behind them, she whispered, 'Did you understand that?'

He stirred in the darkness and cleared his throat. 'I know a number of dialects. They were saying . . . ' He paused as if hesitating to repeat what he had heard. 'They said they have been shooting hostages. Because of my disappearance and because of those men you shot with the Uzi. They think there is another gang of terrorists aboard, of whom they can't find a trace.'

Olive swallowed hard. She wondered which of those she knew might have died as a result of her efforts. She felt she knew how Benjamin must be feeling as he thought about people dying because of him.

'They died for something,' she said at last. 'Not uselessly. Remember that. These people want you for some nefarious purpose, and those who hired me wanted you for something similar. You are like a . . . a weapon in their hands. We had to get you away from them. Who knows what harm might come to a lot more people if they used you?'

He sighed. His hand came across his body and gripped hers. 'Thank you, my dear. You have comforted me.'

Dawes grunted. 'She's right, you know. The worst thing that can happen is for this kind of creeps to achieve their goals. Still, it's damn hard on the innocent bystanders.'

Olive lay silent for a while, thinking deeply. They could still hear occasional thuds from adjoining storage rooms. Once a girl screamed from the direction of the galleys.

At last the Knit Lady had her thoughts organized. 'Being old is a blessing, in a way,' she said. 'You don't hold onto life as desperately as you did when you were younger. At least I don't. If I die today or tomorrow, I'll go content that I did my best with what I had to work with.

'If I'd been obsessed with staying alive, I would still be scrubbing floors at the U.N. or someplace much like it. Keeping body and soul together, just barely, and plodding along.'

She felt Dawes reach across her other side and lay his hand on those already clasped in her lap. 'But I wanted more. I wanted to do something useful with the time I had left. Maybe it sounds crazy, totally immoral to those who care a lot about conventional morality, but a lot of people need to be killed for the public good. I've never killed a single one that I didn't think was better out of the world than in it.'

She could feel her companions' interest, and she went on, 'I've never taken on a job that didn't seem to have merit. Like this one; until I got to know Benjamin I thought he might deserve a time in captivity, just to make him humble.

'Once I realized that wasn't true, I resigned the commission, unofficially of course, but I never take money until the job is done. I don't feel guilty about taking it or about turning it down.' The darkness about them felt almost web-like in its intensity, and she coughed quietly.

'Maybe I'm completely wrong. Maybe I'm not a whit better than any other hit man. I've done a lot of thinking and soul-searching since I carried my vendetta to Francesco's uncle, but I haven't found in my heart that I'm entirely wrong. Unorthodox, of course, but I always had the potential for that.' She paused and stirred uneasily.

'What do you two think?'

'As one who has operated both legally and extralegally,' Scarlatt said, 'I find you responsible and thoughtful. In the half-world I used to inhabit — in which you still live — there are no absolutes, no hard and fast rules, and no rights and wrongs to guide you. You have to write your own scenarios, literally, and I cannot say that I find you culpable.'

'Damn right,' said Dawes. 'You're dealing with people who would kill you as easily as they'd swat a fly. No conception of morality or ethics or anything else. How do you deal with that kind except on their own terms?

'Most are better off dead than alive, and the world is better without them. We'll probably have to send several more to glory before we get out of this too. Let people talk about civil rights and the rights of criminals all they want to, but if you and Benjamin and I didn't do the dirty work, they'd live in a lot worse world than the one we have.'

He laughed softly. 'You got me onto my soapbox. Let that be a warning to you.'

They sat silently then, listening hard to the dark spaces around them. The search had moved to a greater distance, and all they could hear was the creak and groan of the ship and the throb of its engines.

Olive's watch hands seemed stuck in place, time moved so slowly. They ate a bit from Dawes's rations, drank some water, but they didn't stir out of their cubby. The demands of nature had to wait, uncomfortable though it was, until it was safe to move again.

They had grown so accustomed to the moving ship, the muted sounds of water against the hull, that they didn't notice them any longer. Now they waited in darkness, lulled by subtle stirrings and shiftings and creakings, growing drowsy.

Half asleep, Olive leaned her head against Benjamin. Then she tensed and woke fully.

With a series of odd sounds, the ship seemed to falter. The constant grinding of the propeller shaft, not too far beneath them, stopped amid cracklings and groanings.

The *Victorine* slowed in the water and they could tell she was no longer under power.

Dawes switched on his flashlight. Olive saw two faces staring back at her that were probably as pale and bewildered as her own.

She sighed. What now?

32

AXE: REPLY SOONEST

VICTORINE PROPS FOULED WITH NETS. BOARDING PARTIES IN PLACE. WILL GO ABOARD 1130 HOURS UNLESS OTHERWISE ORDERED.

MONARCH REPORTS TWO MORE BODIES IN WATER.
   HACKSAW

Axe sighed and crumpled the message in his hand. What a mess. What a hell of a mess. He had to take it as a sign never to consider any assignment as being routine and without danger, however long he continued his work.

Where was Dawes? His was not, at last report, one of the bodies picked up by *Monarch*. He was an experienced hand, able to care for himself handily, leg or no leg. The thought that he might be spiked

243

to the wall with ice picks, like the unfortunate steward, kept recurring, but Axe kept pushing it away.

He had more pressing concerns at the moment. He lifted the telephone bearing the Presidential seal. After a short wait, the familiar voice said, 'Axe?'

'Yes, Sir. The vessel is presently dead in the water. The boarding parties are in position and will board just before midnight, unless the order is counter-manded. Have you been in touch with the Liberians?'

There was a grunt at the other end of the line. 'As usual, they have washed their hands of the entire affair. Registering vessels is a national industry for them, and they have no interest in the ships themselves or in their crews and passengers. We're clear there.'

'Have your people been able to locate the real owners?'

'It required quite a search, but we found those who own the consortium that owns the parent company that owns the company of record. Guess who?' The President sounded oddly cheerful.

'The Brokers.' Axe had felt that in his bones.

'Exactly. It means they won't object too strenuously to anything we find it necessary to do. We've been gaining on those people for months now, and we already have enough documented evidence to squeeze their Board of Directors hard enough to stifle any squeak they might want to make.'

Axe felt his stomach ease a bit. 'That's good. Then we go ahead? People are going to die, you know.'

The President grunted again. 'People have already died, and more will if we don't act. I've been in touch with France and Great Britain. We've all lost people, according to first identifications. They are agreed that it can hardly be worse.'

'Sir, I have a man in place on the *Victorine*. I am pretty certain he hasn't been found. He's good. He can see through a brick wall — or walk through it, for that matter. He may be able to save some lives. There's some hope of that anyway.'

'It's a nice thought, Axe. I will comfort myself with it while we wait for news.'

The line clicked. Axminster set his instrument back in place and stared for a moment at the photograph of his wife.

Then he transmitted the go-ahead.

For better or for worse.

33

Dawes hadn't joined in the speculations of his companions when the motion of the ship altered and the sound of rushing water against the hull changed its note. He was thinking furiously.

He knew Axe — had known him for twenty years as well as you can get to know someone you work with. He knew the standing orders in situations of this kind. He even knew the approximate locations of the strike forces and minisubs that might be used to recover the *Victorine* from the terrorists.

The fact that people had already been killed, according to what Benjamin overheard, would mean that drastic measures would be taken. Given the proper equipment, he thought, he could have stopped the *Victorine* himself.

At last he spoke. 'They're going to board us. Probably well after dark. I suspect there's been a sub of some kind shadowing us all the way.'

Olive stirred. 'It will mean more deaths. Those old women used to irritate the life out of me, but I'd hate to see any of them killed. We should do something. We're armed to some extent and are free to move around, very cautiously.'

'They're looking high and low for us,' cautioned Scarlatt in a dry tone.

'What time is it?' Dawes asked. 'My damn watch has stopped.'

Olive held the luminous dial of her watch close to her eyes. 'Six o'clock. Still broad daylight. If I were running that operation, I'd wait until very late. Dawn comes early in summer, so midnight would be just about right.'

Dawes drew a deep breath. 'Yes, we've got to get out of here and do what we can find to do. About dark maybe. A couple more hours.'

Olive stirred. 'You and Benjamin can stay put here until dark. I can wander up, looking old and helpless and confused, and they'll just stick me in with the rest of the old ladies and never really think about me at all. You know it and I know it.

'With my knitting bag, I'm armed. I have one of those plastic automatics in there, with yarn wound around the parts, and I'm going to put it together as soon as I can. I really think I should go topside and get into position. I might be able to save somebody.'

'You might get killed! Scarlatt exploded. 'My dear lady, do you understand the risk you're taking?'

Olive chuckled quietly. 'Benjamin, you'd think I was some sweet, little tea-party type who'd never done anything more exciting than pruning a rosebush. I have been hijacked before, I'll have you know. And got out alive and unsuspected.'

'Then you know how dangerous it could get up there.'

Dawes turned on the flash and stared at Olive in the pale glare. 'Canada Air? Three years ago?'

She grinned into the light. 'Right on. I was on my way to . . . do a bit of business.'

Scarlatt's head came up. 'Three years ago? That's when Melmark was assassinated in Toronto, and we all sighed with relief.'

'Actually, that was my business. I was on my way, all innocent and wigged and made up to look sweet and doddery. Pictures of grandchildren, lilac scented handkerchief, the whole thing. Just before we entered the landing pattern over Toronto, Jacques Chasin and another man grabbed the stewardess and ordered the pilot to head for Ottawa. Only God knows what they intended to do there.'

'I remember that there was a lot of confusion after the plane landed,' Dawes said. 'Nobody knew exactly what had happened to those hijackers. They were just dead.'

She chuckled again. 'I had to go to the john. I can look terribly upset and uncomfortable, about to wet my pants, you know. Chasin sent the other man with me. I made ugly noises for a minute. Then I unfastened the door and begged the hijacker for help.

'When he stuck his head inside, I put a knitting needle through his eyeball into his brain.'

Scarlatt drew a sharp breath, but he said nothing.

'Then I settled him against the bulkhead beside the toilet in as lifelike a position as I could manage and went tottering forward, covered with blood and sobbing that I was hemorrhaging.

'Chasin was behind the last row of passengers, holding the stew in front of him and facing forward. He turned when he heard me and was flustered when he saw the state I was in. I got him beneath the girl's arm with the needle, directly in the heart. The stew fainted, which gave me time to wash, take a seat at the rear, turn my sweater inside-out, take off the wig, wipe my face, and become just another hysterical passenger.'

Olive felt suddenly tired and old. 'Nobody had seen anything, for I sat in the rear to begin with. Everyone crowded up front when the plane had landed at last, and nobody could tell one of us from the other. All the blood was inside my sweater, and my face and hands were clean. At the very end, I had to go to the john in the terminal.'

She grinned. 'Nobody denies an old lady the right to do that. When I came out, most had gone and I was somebody else entirely.'

Dawes clicked off the flash. 'I think you're right,' he said. 'You can handle yourself. Nobody knows anything at all about you, and God knows, you don't look dangerous. No more than a coral snake does.'

She felt a surge of relief. 'I knew you'd see it. Here, help me put this ridiculous pistol together.'

She offered balls of yarn to each, and they sat in the darkness, winding off the invisible red strands onto fresh balls, freeing the plastic parts of the gun. When they were all ready, Dawes lit the flash again and assembled the weapon with speed and assurance.

'I've carried these babies through airline checks more than once,' he said. 'Where's your ammo?'

She fumbled a small metal box marked HEART MEDICINE from the bottom of her knitting bag. 'Here. Thirty rounds. I hope that's enough.'

She stood as straight as possible in the cramped space and pulled her sweater straight, brushed dust from her jeans, and straightened her hair. The curls she'd used as a disguise had gone limp, and she screwed her gray mop into a severe knot on top of her head, skewering it in place with three huge hairpins from her bag.

Dawes boosted her over the barrier and remained to listen to her almost inaudible passage through the untidy maze of crates. When he turned back, Benjamin was cursing softly. When he paused for breath, Dawes said, 'It's hurt pride, my friend. Not to worry. That's one tough little broad.'

34

The hunt for those evanescent fugitives had moved into other areas of the ship, as Olive crept through quiet passages to the companionway and listened hard before beginning to climb. Luck was with her. She made it to the main deck before meeting anyone, and she was well away from both elevators and companionway by that time.

She had donned her senile persona before setting out, and she moved toward the dark-skinned young woman with the Uzi as if finding a long-lost friend.

'Oh, help me. I've been hiding, and I'm so hungry and thirsty. I don't remember where my cabin is either. Please help me find it!'

The woman glared at her, obviously not understanding anything except her over-wrought tone. She gestured with her weapon, herding Olive toward the main lounge, where the Knit Lady joined a huddle of elderly women, few of whom she recognized and none of whom she knew well.

They looked up without interest as she settled into a chair and took out her knitting. Some were also doing handwork, without paying much attention to their stitches. Some stared at the wall and wept quietly. The extremely fat woman next to her turned after a bit and really looked at her.

'They're going to kill us all,' she said in a conversational tone. 'The man told us. That Blivens fellow — I never liked him at all. Too many teeth. He was with these animals all along, pretending to care for us and planning to do . . . this. I told my . . . husband . . . ' Tears welled into her eyes and she choked back sobs.

Olive put her hand on the woman's arm. 'Your husband? Is he all right?'

'He's dead. They shot him with the first lot. They threw them all overboard. Blivens said it was because we helped somebody get away from them. I think they meant that distinguished-looking Englishman, but we aren't certain. They don't make much sense.'

Olive felt a brief pang of guilt. She had, she felt, killed all those people. If she had left Benjamin in the hands of his guards . . . but she pushed the thought aside. That was not the way these things worked. They would have killed some anyway. Death was, after all, only a short time in the futures of most of those aboard the *Victorine*.

She probably wouldn't live out the night herself, no matter what she had led her companions to believe. Her reflexes were not what they had been. There were a lot of terrorists, all well armed, young, and vicious. Do what she might, she was only a lone old woman and the odds were stacked against her.

'What a pity,' she said, in the tone of the silly woman she seemed. Olive understood the fortunes of war, and this woman's husband had been a casualty in its first battle.

In a short while, a harried-looking girl in white brought sandwiches to the lounge and passed them around with foam cups of coffee. The women ate every crumb, which told Olive that food came infrequently and undependably.

It was almost dark now, the sea gleaming restlessly beneath the stars. She stared through the dimly lit glass of the lounge window, seeing herself and the others as tenuous ghosts superimposed on the darker image of the sea.

'I'm so tired,' she sighed.

The fat woman roused from her thoughts. 'Make yourself comfortable. This is where we stay all the time. They don't let us go to our cabins any more. There are blankets folded up under the couches. Here . . . ' She bent with a loud grunt and pulled a dark blue blanket from beneath Olive's seat.

'Thank you.' Olive put her knitting into her bag and felt the pistol's shape beneath the concealment of the half-finished muffler.

Hands hidden by the blanket, she transferred the gun to the waistband of her jeans, hidden beneath her baggy sweater.

No guard was set over the women in the lounge. One of the terrorists checked on them from time to time, counting heads, making sure nobody wandered away. Olive checked her watch every time this happened, and they were using fifteen-minute intervals.

The ship was quiet, rolling with the waves and making no headway. Occasional sharp comments or commands from those patrolling the deck came to her ears, but Olive was listening past those sounds. She was trying to hear stealthy oars lapping into the sea, the slipping of quiet keels through the water, toward the *Victorine*.

Time crawled. Ten. Ten-thirty. Eleven. Eleven-thirty. The guards came and went regularly, bad habit though she knew it to be. Predictable. At eleven-thirty, the guard who came did not return to join his fellows. Olive maneuvered the body into the place she had occupied on a couch, covered it with a blanket, and slid into the shadows behind the cluster of chairs and couches.

If help didn't come, they were all in trouble, but that was true anyway. Hidden, she waited for some sign that a new element had entered the situation. That was why she heard the faint thud of a boat against the *Victorine*'s hull.

She held her breath. Then she rose silently and shook the eight women, one by one, into wakefulness. 'Hide back here, behind the couches. Hurry!' she whispered.

Mabel, the fat lady, didn't fit behind any of the couches. The space was too narrow, and the couches were fastened to the floor. Olive, determined to salvage this one if possible, found a serving area with a stout door. Into that she crammed poor Mabel, with orders to fasten the door and not to open it again until someone who sounded dependable asked her to.

She rolled all the blankets into as lifelike postures as possible, managing to counterfeit sleeping shapes scattered about the dimly lit lounge. All the while she heard stealthy sounds from the deck, from below, from the decks above. Once her ear was attuned to that secret activity, it seemed to drown out everything else.

That was why a sudden burst of fire

from automatic weapons made her jump. She raised her head to stare over the back of a chair, and one of the enemy tumbled through the outer door, turned and fired in the direction from which he had come.

She shot him in the back of the head, and the women behind the couches shrieked thinly.

'Shut up! I shot him, not you. Now be still,' she commanded, and they subsided.

She felt a tug at her elbow. It was the quiet Jewish lady, whose terrified gaze had clung to every one of the terrorists who came.

Now she looked as if she were waking from a nightmare. Her eyes were bright and black in the faint light. 'He has a gun. I'll get it,' she said. Without waiting for Olive to agree, she crawled across the carpet to the sprawled body.

Without wincing at the blood, she tumbled him over and reached for his Uzi. She looked at it for a moment. Then she searched the body for ammunition, returning to Olive's side with his entire supply.

'Welcome aboard,' murmured the Knit

Lady. 'Do you know how to handle that?'

'I was in the Army in Israel, back in the old days,' she said. 'I learned to shoot just about anything.'

'This is an automatic,' Olive said, 'if you'd feel more comfortable handling that.'

'Yes, I would.' The woman pushed the Uzi toward her. 'Do you know how to use this one?'

Olive nodded and took the weapon gratefully. It was worth a hundred handguns. With it, she just might keep this bunch alive until help arrived.

Her attention, which had turned to immediate problems, now returned to the larger one. She could hear shouts, gunfire running steps. Many steps, in fact, came in her direction. She laid her arm across the back of the chair and aimed the weapon to cover the door.

Four combat-fatigued shapes dashed into the lounge. Not one looked toward the supposedly sleeping women. She sprayed a burst that took them all down. Another silenced those who still groaned. A feeble cheer rose from behind the couches.

The Jewish woman smiled at Olive. 'I am Miriam,' she said. 'Shall I get those too?'

'Be my guest,' said the Knit Lady.

Again Miriam crawled toward the door, though this time it took her longer. There were more bodies to search, but she returned with four automatics, another Uzi, and a bag of grenades.

Olive moved across the room and touched a panel that dimmed the lights to darkness. The corridor outside was softly lighted, and now it appeared bright by contrast with the dark lounge.

When she was again behind the line of couches, she turned into the darkness and asked, 'Does anyone know how to handle a gun, besides Miriam?'

There came a stirring in the blackness. 'I can shoot. I haven't done it in years, and I used to think guns were ungodly, but I know how. Somehow, in this situation, I think I wouldn't have any problem with killing one of these beasts.'

A hand fumbled forward, and Olive put an automatic into it. 'Watch it. The recoil makes your finger tighten and fire it

262

again, if you don't keep control.'

'Don't worry. I know how,' said the wispy voice.

Three more hands came forward to take weapons. Nobody knew how to handle the Uzi, and Olive was just as glad. Those things could kill a friend as easily as an enemy. When all those who would accept weapons were armed, Olive stood up.

'I need to see if I can help somebody else. Can you handle it here?' she asked.

Miriam's quiet voice replied, 'We will protect ourselves. Go and help anyone you can. We are no longer helpless victims, like my father was at Auschwitz.'

'Good for you. And good luck!'

Olive listened intently before going into the corridor. When she went, she did it with a rush and a roll, her arthritic knee giving her hell all the way. But there was no one there, though quite a firefight seemed to be going on out on deck.

She headed in that direction. Might as well be killed for a goat as a sheep, she thought.

35

Dawes and Scarlatt eased out of their hiding place at the first sound of gunfire above-decks. Distant as it was, it sounded flat, like firecrackers in some innocent celebration. Armed with the Uzi and Dawes's automatic, they crept along the corridors to the galleys.

'Might as well clear it out down here,' Dawes said. 'Anyone who fights his way this far is going to have hell, with all those hostages in there.'

Scarlatt nodded. They fell to either side and Dawes kicked in the door, knowing how reckless it was. The armed guard, set to watch the kitchen workers, started up, brought up his weapon, and froze. The Uzi out-stared him without difficulty.

The men and women staffing the galleys and the dining rooms were huddled together on makeshift pallets, wherever there was floor space. They rose, bewildered, to find their captor in the process of being efficiently bound with strips of tablecloth and apron.

The chef, very young and excitable, was a Greek named Ektor. He took charge of the guard's weapon, promising to hold the galleys against any return of the terrorists, while taking care not to shoot anyone not garbed in the inevitable combat fatigues.

'We have much weapon here,' he said, gesturing widely with the cleaver in his left hand. 'We have knife, rolling pin. Much we have to kill them, if they come. You not worry. We are fine now.'

They took him at his word.

The corridors at this level were still and quiet. The two risked using the freight elevator, which carried them silently up to the lower deck. There they left it and went out into the salty damp of the night air.

It was noisy on deck. The boarding party must have come aboard aft of the elevators, and at least some were pinned down by rapid-fire weapons. Dawes handed Scarlatt the Uzi, regained his automatic, and flattened against the floor, to slide away like a snake, leaving Scarlatt to cover him.

The older man crept along behind as Dawes reconnoitered. They gained the uncovered portion of the deck, where flashes marked the perimeter of the fire-fight.

Scarlatt shouted in English, 'Heads down, lads! We're scorching them.'

Dawes hoped they took him at his word, as Benjamin opened up with the Uzi, sweeping an arc of fire some three feet above the level of the deck. Dawes picked off individual shapes in the foreground. Then he clicked on his flash, which showed a line of men lying flat and twitching amid their own blood. Beyond those, a half-dozen black-clad shapes rose and came forward.

'Thanks,' said an American voice.

Dawes turned off his light. 'There are possibly groups of hostages on all three decks. We must go and see if we can locate them. 'Good luck!'

He felt Benjamin's hand on his elbow, and they melted together into the darkness before the others could say anything else.

'The main deck,' Dawes said. 'That's where the least disabled and the wealthiest were put. That's where we'll find most of the hostages, I suspect.'

The game room was the first place they found that was dimly lit and guarded by nervous custodians. Scarlatt moaned, muttering in dialect, 'Help me! Comrades, I've been wounded.'

No one came out, which didn't surprise Dawes. These people were not concerned with anyone's life or welfare, even their own. He heard Scarlatt scratch feebly at the door, pushing against it as he lay flat on the deck.

A step sounded inside. Someone stood over the Englishman, the outline of a weapon glinting in his hand. Dawes shot the man, who had already aimed the weapon at Scarlatt's head, and they dived together into the room he had just left.

Heads came up from improvised pillows on the floor. A woman whimpered, but someone hushed her.

'How many are there here?' asked Scarlatt.

'I think twelve,' came the reply from a

frail old fellow, who hardly looked strong enough to speak.

'Is it possible to barricade this door?' Dawes asked. 'With the guard dead, you might be safe if you can do that.'

'We'll turn the billiard table on its side and push it against the door. We can brace it with chairs, I think,' the old fellow said.

'Good. We'll see if someone else needs help.' Dawes was already moving into the corridor again.

Twice they liberated rooms filled with oldsters. Once they arrived too late. Four bodies lay on the floor in plain sight, and they suspected that others might be behind the scramble of tables and chairs.

Dawes could hear the newcomers now moving all through the vessel, sudden bursts of gunfire marking their routes. He was glad the skirmishes seemed to be growing fewer.

'The game seems to be over,' said Scarlatt, just as he and Dawes rounded a corner and stepped into the middle of an unexpected ambush. A slug took Benjamin in the leg, and he toppled.

Dawes went down too, but he had hit the deck voluntarily. The two rolled behind a lifeboat davit, which gave very little protection, and fired back blindly.

From behind their attackers there cane a sudden blast. Shrapnel whined past them, twanging off metal of rail and davit. For a short moment there was no sound except for groans. Dawes flicked on his flash again.

A grenade, he was certain, had shattered the small group that had pinned them down. 'That was a grenade,' Scarlatt muttered, as he wriggled over to examine one of the bodies.

But Dawes was staring into the dimness. 'I thought I saw Olive,' he said. 'Going off toward the other side of the ship.'

'Olive!' Scarlatt shouted.

'Olive!' Dawes roared.

But there was no reply.

36

Olive heard the commotion ahead of her and moved silently up on the group of terrorists. They had someone pinned down by the rail, and anyone they were trying to kill had to be a friend of hers. She rolled a grenade toward them, the sound lost amid the rattle of gunfire.

She ducked behind the corner just in time. The roar of the blast almost deafened her. Noisy things, grenades, she thought, but handy at times.

Olive was now almost certain the ship was in friendly hands. She'd avoided groups of black-clad troops, who usually herded blood-stained terrorists before them. Now seemed to be an excellent time for the Knit Lady to disappear from view.

She wondered how well guarded were the craft in which those troops arrived, but she put that out of her mind. They would be well secured, she felt certain.

Still, it didn't hurt to check them out. Olive moved to the quieter side of the vessel and accustomed her eyes to the shifting gleams and shadows of the waves below. A small craft bulked dark against the starlit water. Voices spoke there, and she listened intently. No hope there, she realized.

It was a silly notion, anyway. She moved along the deck, almost beneath the rail, scanning the water below until something caught her eye. Another dark blot was there, not secured to the side. It was moving toward the *Victorine* in silence, cloaked by the darkness, any sound hidden by the noises aboard the embattled ship.

Was it reinforcing the first group of rescuers? That seemed unnecessary, she thought. Might it be help for the terrorists? Or even other terrorists entirely?

Olive flattened her self against the deck, cursing the damp and her arthritis with equal vigor. The craft bumped gently against the hull. There was no sound aboard, no hail, no whisper that it was there at all. It was now obvious that the *Victorine* had been retaken, for lights had been turned on aft, and the riding lights

271

were again burning. There was no good reason why these newcomers should be so stealthy.

She crawled along the deck, hugging the shadows under the bulkheads, keeping an eye on that vessel hidden under the curve of the *Victorine*'s hull. A head — hooded — came over the rail. The hood was marked with a symbol she recognized. Dammit, she'd known the Brokers were involved in this, almost from the beginning.

She scooted across the deck on her belly and thrust a knitting needle with scientific accuracy between two ribs of the boarder. The hooded shape gave a quiet gurgle and dropped back into the boat.

A muffled exclamation met his arrival, and while those below were presumably trying to find out what had gone wrong, Olive pulled the pin of one of her grenades and dropped it over the side into the smaller craft. She hugged the deck and heard debris pass over her on its way upward.

I hope I didn't hole the hull of the

Victorine, she thought. She pulled another pin and dropped another grenade.

Then she got the hell out of there.

Staying in her own cabin was out of the question, she knew, but she visited it briefly and brought away everything she might need. She found a quiet spot in one of the storage rooms below and changed her clothing.

Now she was dressed in a light cotton print, expensive but undistinguished. Flat shoes managed to make her legs look warped and crippled. A wig turned her gray bun into a hennaed crop, and makeup to match turned her into an over-age houri, on the make at a most unbecoming age. She worked for a bit on finding the most idiotic expression compatible with being allowed out without a keeper.

Her knitting bag turned inside out to become an expensive tapestry handbag, and all its contents were zipped into pockets in the lining. She found an empty cabin and a mirror and examined herself carefully. Her own husband would never have known her.

When the *Victorine* docked, she waited

until the rush of reporters and relieved family members dwindled. Then she walked past Dawes and Scarlatt, who seemed to have been wounded, as he was sitting in a wheelchair and looking very pale. As she made her way onto the wharf, neither gave her a second glance.

Olive felt sad to leave them concerned about her safety, but no matter how one trusted people during the stress of danger, it was better not to put them to any hard tests. She made that a rule in life, and it was too late in her career to break it now.

She might die tomorrow, or she might live another decade. She didn't intend to do either in prison.

37

Kim Dawes limped up the steps of Axe's townhouse and tapped at the door. He was feeling fit again, though still sore in every bone and muscle. Such activity as he had been driven to in the past week would have been hard on him even fifteen years ago. At this stage in his life it had been stressful, to say the least.

The door opened. It was Tape, retired now. He smiled at her and greeted his old chum, then followed her down the corridor.

Where would they go this time? The greenhouse room? But it was yet another room, this one small and intimate. A parlor, perhaps, for some lady who liked luxury in a small space. The portrait of a middle-aged woman hung above the shell-shaped fireplace.

Axe sat in his usual abandoned attitude before the fireplace, though it was entirely too hot for the hearth to hold a blaze. The older man looked up as Dawes entered. He seemed gray and weary. Lines Drillbit had never seen before were etched deeply into his face.

'Don't tell me you worried about me,' he said, leaning forward to shake Axe's extended hand. 'Don't you know you can't get rid of a bad penny that easily? Just do me a favour — don't DO me any more favours. No more milk runs, all right? The old bod just isn't up to it any longer.'

Axminster laughed softly. 'You did make me sweat, I'll admit. And we never did find out what the steward wanted us to know, though it's pretty easy to guess, after all that happened to that cruise.'

'I suspect it had to do with the intended hijacking. But what proof have we that it was the thing he might have warned us about?' Dawes asked.

'Don't,' moaned Axe. 'Another go like that one and I'll be fit for a nursing home.'

Dawes settled into a chair and accepted a glass of iced tea from Tape. 'What is most interesting is that other strike force, the one that tried to board soon after ours had things in hand. Nobody aboard that craft survived, but there were bodies galore, floating all over the place. Our minisub was certain another underwater craft was lurking close by, all the time they shadowed us. The vessel itself was owned by an outfit on Crete.'

Axe looked at him sharply. 'How did it happen to explode?' he asked. 'No one ever explained that to me, though reports have come in from all directions. Nobody admits to having blown it up. No one knew it was there until it did blow up. I can see no reason why it blew at all. What in heaven's name did happen?'

Dawes took a long sip of the cold tea. Tape had laced it with something much stronger, and he appreciated the thought as the liquid went down. He set the glass on the table beside him and leaned back in the deep chair.

'I believe it was our Knit Lady,' he said. 'She was certain it was the Brokers who hired her to abduct Benjamin Scarlatt. She had rejected the commission, once she saw the further orders attached to the originals, though she had not informed them of that.' He sighed.

'She was around all through the taking of the ship. A lounge full of old ladies thought the description we gave them sounded like the woman who killed their guards and armed them, leaving them to defend themselves, which they did quite effectively. I never saw so many sweet old ladies armed with so many very ugly weapons. They used them, too, more than once, while they waited for relief and rescue. There were five or six bodies outside the door to the lounge.'

'But what makes you think the Knit Lady destroyed that other vessel?'

'Because she had a bag of hand grenades. A nice lady named Miriam Neufeld told me all about that. One of the terrorists the unknown lady killed had it on his belt. Miriam retrieved them, with his weapon and other ammunition.

'She gave them to the one who might have been Olive. When Scarlatt and I were under fire out on deck, someone sent a grenade into the middle of the bunch that had us pinned down. Blew them to Kingdom Come. So I know one old lady had grenades, and I know the landing craft was riddled with grenade fragments, as were the bodies in and around it.

'Who else could it have been?'

'And she just disappeared without any trace?'

Dawes frowned. 'There's no way she could have left the ship. She wasn't stupid enough to try to swim to safety with a life jacket. She didn't pass Scarlatt and me, for we waited on the dock until every last living soul came off the *Victorine*. Not a person who remotely resembled her came off that ship.

'We went aboard again with some men and searched until our knees buckled, and we found not a single trace of anyone.'

'The little woman who wasn't there,' mused Axe. 'The Brokers are in disarray,' he added. 'There has been an upset of some kind in their hierarchy. The Chairman, whoever he may be, seems to be in disfavour. It makes me wonder how our little friend will fare when they get their act together again. She did, as far as they know, fail to accomplish her mission.'

Dawes stared at his hands and wondered. 'Don't think I'm not worried about that. She was a friend, Axe. She pitched right in and helped with that dead steward, without asking a question. When the going got toughest, she was right there. I know she saved Scarlatt and me, there at the last. I worry about her a lot.'

Axminster twisted to look up at the portrait of his late wife. 'You've never been married, have you, Dawes?'

'No, I haven't.'

'Men get in the habit of thinking of women as fragile and helpless. I think you're wasting a lot of energy worrying about that one.'

He looked back at Dawes. 'If she's the woman Laura was, she will handle everything without turning a hair.'

Dawes finished his tea and stood. 'I hope you're right. I wish I could accept that, but I'll always wonder about her.'

Axe laughed, a sharp bark. 'I'm afraid you'll never find out,' he said. 'Not if she's the person she seems to be. We used her once, you know, and I always thought she was a man. Now we know.'

38

The silver-grey Lincoln slid to a stop before the portico of the big house. The sun was warm, the leaves were beginning to turn, and the big man who was helped from the car looked about him with appreciation.

'It's good to be home again,' he said.

Corrigan said nothing, though he looked a bit surprised. Gianello seldom confided such things to his underlings. He felt a bit embarrassed at having done so, now, even though he had hated his stay in the hospital.

Julius, the new butler, met them at the door. 'Your room is ready, Sir, if you would like to lie down. Or there is a small fire in your study, if you would rather go there.'

Gianello felt an unfamiliar pleasure. Such thought for his comfort was something he had never really considered, but it was a pleasant thing. Perhaps he'd had his mind too firmly on business, all these years. He hadn't taken time to enjoy the small niceties that money obtained so easily.

'Thank you, Julius. I'll go to the study. You may bring me something to eat. I wasn't hungry at noon. Something . . . ' — he grimaced — ' . . . bland.'

'Indeed, Sir. We do have a new cook, who seems an excellent woman. She is no gourmet chef, but she does a wonderful job of plain cooking. Until we can find a better one, I think she'll do. She specializes in soups and really fine puddings. Just the ticket for you, at this point, I should think.'

Under Gianello's expansiveness, Julius was growing almost voluble. His employer smiled, an even greater concession. 'I would like to meet her. Until they get my digestion repaired, we might as well keep her. We can always cater anything fancy.'

'I'll send her in with your meal, Sir. You may find her somewhat elderly and not at all beautiful, but she seems to be a solid sort, as far as I can tell.'

'Old and ugly is best,' Gianello chuckled. 'The young and beautiful ones get married and leave us.'

Julius ventured a laugh. To his astonishment his employer joined him.

Corrigan supported Gianello into the study, while Julius solicitously opened doors, poked up the fire, and fluffed the cushion of his chair. Gianello sank into the padded seat with a sigh of satisfaction.

'Give me five minutes to get my breath,' he said. 'Then send in the cook, if she has the food ready.'

'We thought you might be hungry, Sir. She has everything waiting for you.'

Gianello closed his eyes as the door whispered shut behind Corrigan. It was, indeed, good to be home. What did it matter if he was to be deposed as Chairman of the Brokers? He had more money than he could spend if he lived ten lifetimes.

He opened his eyes and sat straighter. What had come over him? Illness was no excuse for such weakness. He had already disposed of most of those involved in his recent fiasco. Contracts were out on the rest. He was going to cover his tracks so well that nobody would be able to bring up anything definite in order to pry him from his position.

He touched the bell. He was hungry. It was easier to plan sudden deaths on a full stomach.

A very neat but elderly woman entered at once, carrying a covered tray. She set it on a side table and deftly set his small window-side table with china, linen, silver, glass. A fragrant tureen of soup emerged from beneath a silver cover. A plate of crisp toast joined it, along with a cupful of pudding with bananas sliced on top.

'It's like going back to my babyhood,' he grumbled, swivelling his chair to face his food. He turned to glance at her sideways. 'And what is your name?' he asked her.

The woman smiled. It lit up her face, a strangely young face, though well worn and full of character.

'I was born Olive Shaughnessy,' she said in a deep and rather beautiful voice. 'I married a Rienzi, but I am better known as the Knit Lady.'

The words didn't penetrate his mind for a moment. In that time, she moved very close to him. Too close — he pushed the chair back, reached for the button that called Corrigan.

'I cut the wire,' she said. 'When you put out contracts, you should have chosen your victims more carefully. Nobody assassinates the Knit Lady.'

There was a steely glint as her hand emerged from beneath her apron. He half rose, but his recent illness had made him slow. He couldn't avoid her, and he couldn't fight her.

The needle punctured his heart, but he hardly felt it. He was staring desperately into those amazingly blue eyes. How had he missed that electric blueness when he first saw her?

And then he was dead.

★ ★ ★

Nobody came into the study for a half hour. By that time Olive was gone without a trace.

A walk down a mountain, through a forest, was no great feat for the Knit Lady.

39

Dawes was unlocking his door when the telephone inside his apartment began ringing. Cursing, he dashed in, flung his briefcase on the couch, and caught up the receiver.

'Drillbit,' he answered, from long habit.

'Dawes, you've never really reconciled yourself to a desk job, now have you?' It was Axminster, chuckling fruitily.

'Oh, Axe. I haven't heard from you for a while. Thought you'd finally turned me out to my paper-ridden pasture.'

'I've been thinking about that. Maybe company policy is a bit behind the times. Thinking about that lady you knew a while ago too. It seems to us that if a woman of her years, with arthritis yet, can get about and do as much as she managed to do, there might still be a bit of kick in the old Drillbit. What do you think?'

'I think that one day I may shoot my desk — and me — to get us both out of our misery,' Dawes replied.

'I thought as much. We've had a request from Interior. It seems there's been something of a flap in the Brokerage. It's a good time to look closely into that entire set-up. Would you be interested? It might turn out to be as dangerous as your recent cruise.'

Dawes grinned at the wall. 'I'd love it.'

'Yes, I thought you would. Oh, and Drillbit . . . about that lady. Would it interest you to know how the Brokers came to be in such disarray?'

Dawes frowned. 'How?'

'We don't know who, of course, but Gianello — yes, that one — was killed at his home yesterday. A stab wound, immediately fatal, delivered with something very long and sharp. A recently hired cook seems to be under suspicion. No apparent motive.'

Dawes's grin stretched until his cheeks hurt. 'Have they caught her?'

'Of course not. She has gone without a trace.'

'I'll give you ten to one,' Dawes chuckled, 'that she has gone on another damned cruise.'

Epilogue

The Hollies
August 3

My Dear Weathering,

If this was a rest cure, I wonder what you would prescribe for excitement? Seldom, even in my active days, have I been pushed nearer to my limits.

The wound in my leg is healing nicely, and the local man you recommended seems more than competent. The rest of me seems, strangely enough, to be in much better shape than I was when I embarked on this geriatric adventure.

Your abject apologies have been accepted, though they were totally unnecessary. This was exactly what I needed to do for my health. While I will not, of course, return to active duty, I have learned not to allow myself to be shunted aside into a passive role.

Do not, I beg of you, continue to blame yourself for the exigencies of my trip. I enjoyed them all.

If Challoner queries you with regard to my fitness, I expect you to confirm that I am quite able to do anything I judge to be within my competency. I have decided that only my own assessment of my condition matters. I expect to return to semi-active duty soon, and much of it can be done here at home. I would not dream of blackmailing you into backing me on this, but do you recall the small matter of the Dean's Rolls? I do.

Best regards,
Benjamin

★ ★ ★

The Hollies
August 3

My Dear Challoner,
By now you have had time to read my report thoroughly and to think about its implications. If someone like

me is vulnerable to that sort of use by terrorists or other groups, then others may be as well. It is something to consider carefully, though in a free society it is hard to think what may lawfully be done to circumvent it.

I expect to return to work somewhat more actively than in past years. The leg is healing nicely. I find myself very fit, in contrast to my condition before my voyage. I believe that Hugh Weathering will bear me out in this. Expect me soon.

I appreciate your recommendation that I take the recent cruise. A most interesting and enlightening experience. Perhaps I shall take another one day, though I hardly expect to find such helpful companions again.

My regards to your charming Hildegarde.

Scarlatt

★　★　★

The Hollies
August 3

My Dearest Louise,

Our brief reunion in London was too full of emotion for expression, I fear. The thought that I might never see you and my grandchildren again was the worst aspect of my adventure aboard the *Victorine*. For the rest . . . it made me feel young again.

I am not without aching bones, of course, for that time will not come again. But I am alive and competent, and I had not felt so for a long while. You may not be surprised if I go back to work rather more actively than before.

You have asked me more than once about my little friend Olive. I wish I could tell you what happened to her. I cannot feel she is dead, for her body was never found. I would like to know, myself, how she came through the last night of that affair.

If things had been different — much different — I might well have tried to bring you a late-blooming stepmother.

Not that we ever spoke of such matters, for neither she nor I had time to think about any wintry romance. But now I wish we had. She gave me the sense of being looked after that your mother used to do, and she was totally dependable.

That is a rare quality, in these times.

However we will probably never know what became of her. And I am getting better by the day. Take care, my love, and bring the children to visit during their next holiday.

Your loving father,
Benjamin

* * *

Addressed to:
Colonel B. Scarlatt
The Hollies, Hants.

At sea
August 8

Dear Benjamin,

Although this goes against all my cherished rules, I find I must write to you. The dangers we shared, as well as the wonderful trips and the lazy days on deck, seem to have forged a bond that I cannot ignore.

As you probably suspected, I managed to leave the *Victorine* without being detected. I felt that you and Dawes thought the art of disguise was somewhat silly and amateurish, but I believe I have proved its worth. I walked past both of you on the dock, you in a wheelchair, Dawes watching everything with sharp eyes. Neither of you gave me a second glance.

On my return home, incognito, I found some loose ends that had to be attended to. Once that was done, I found myself wondering what a real cruise would be like, without all the excitement (and invalids) ours contained.

I find it dull. No terrorists. No stewards to dump into the sea. Worst of all, no Dawes and no Benjamin Scarlatt.

However, I manage to stay busy. I have, however, given up knitting. I now crochet.

In retirement, I find that knitting has too many old associations; besides which, it would be a labor of Hercules to assassinate anyone with a crochet hook. I find old instincts remain buried better if they are not tempted by efficient weapons near at or in — hand.

Goodbye, Benjamin. Take care and God speed. I value the memory of our brief acquaintance.

The Knit Lady

We do hope that you have enjoyed reading this large print book.

Did you know that all of our titles are available for purchase?

We publish a wide range of high quality large print books including:
Romances, Mysteries, Classics
General Fiction
Non Fiction and Westerns

Special interest titles available in large print are:
The Little Oxford Dictionary
Music Book, Song Book
Hymn Book, Service Book

Also available from us courtesy of Oxford University Press:
Young Readers' Dictionary
(large print edition)
Young Readers' Thesaurus
(large print edition)

For further information or a free brochure, please contact us at:
Ulverscroft Large Print Books Ltd.,
The Green, Bradgate Road, Anstey,
Leicester, LE7 7FU, England.
Tel: (00 44) **0116 236 4325**
Fax: (00 44) **0116 234 0205**